hunger for death

JOSHUA MARSELLA

ALSO BY JOSHUA MARSELLA

Scratches
Severed

For Jody,

Enjoy my dark tales!
Great to meet you!
STEPHEN KING !!

HUNGER
FOR DEATH

Joshua Marsella (signature)

JOSHUA MARSELLA

HUNGER FOR DEATH
Copyright © 2021 by Joshua Marsella
ISBN: 979-8764255729
First Paperback Edition: November 2021

"A Trailer Park Christmas" previously appeared in *Santa Claws Coming Deathlehem Anthology*; "Sacrifice" previously appeared in *Alien Agenda Publishing Sampler 2020*

Edited by Lydia Prime
Cover art by Neal Auch
Cover design by Freddie Åhlin & Brian Scutt
Interior title art by Don Noble | Rooster Republic Press
Interior formatting by Todd Keisling | Dullington Design Co.

Published by Cold Hands Press

CONTENT WARNING DISCLAIMER

Content warnings located on page 185.
May Contain Spoilers

TABLE OF CONTENTS

This collection is dedicated to horror lovers all over the world.

"The future is uncertain, but the end is always near..."
- Jim Morrison

"...But if I am the Devil's child, I will live then from the Devil."
- Ralph Waldo Emerson

HUNGER
FOR
DEATH

DAPHNE

I've always been a skeptic, but that all changed on the night we lost Daphne."

§

Growing up, I lived on my family's small pig farm in Whitefield. Once I was old enough for chores, it was my job to put the pigs in the barn at night and freshen their water. Simple enough and always uneventful. Sometimes my imagination would get the better of me and I would see things out in the fields that weren't there. I would always chalk it up to my overactive imagination, continue on with my chore, say goodnight to the pigs, then head back inside.

One night in late September, I was running a little late to put the pigs to bed, so I grabbed my flashlight and hurried out to the yard. The stars were beautiful, as they always were a clear night in the country. The darkness among the stars felt infinite.

To my surprise the pig pen was empty. I slid open the heavy barn door, instantly relieved by the sounds of squeals. That familiar scent of hay was a comfort.

Working my way around the barn to change out the water, it occurred to me that my favorite pig I named Daphne was missing. Daphne was our best breeder and I'd grown fond of her for the way she always trudged up to the fence to stick her snout through the gap to greet me. Sometimes I would sneak her part of my candy bar as a special treat since she was worked so hard. The fact that she was pregnant made me warier because her litter was valuable to my family. I called her name and checked around the inside of the barn one more time, but sure enough, she was nowhere to be found.

After I had the rest of the drift settled in for the night, I walked back out to the yard to search for Daphne. It was a chilly evening. I could see the puff of my breath in the beam of the flashlight like a laser and smoke show at a concert. My pulse began to race as I approached the pig pen. It was empty. A peculiar combination of relief and disappointment swept over me. I peered around into the darkness having an uncomfortable feeling of being watched, but nothing was visible outside the rays of the porchlight and my flashlight. All was quiet in the yard.

Boosting myself up onto the bottom board of the fence for a better look, I pointed the flashlight along the fencing that surrounded the pen, but only saw mud, hoof prints, and a scattering of hay. As I circled back one more time, my eyes caught a glimpse of an unexpected flicker of light reflecting the flashlight's beam. A pair of dark almond-shaped eyes stared at me through the gap in the fence, and I chuckled to myself as I thought I'd found Daphne.

I hopped off the fence and walked around to the other side to fetch her from her hiding spot. I called her a silly girl as I rounded the corner, then gasped, nearly stopping my heart.

A petite, thin figure resembling a child turned and glared at me with what I can only describe as a look of pure animosity. Its knees and elbows were bulbous joints of bone and skin. Its enormous head looked too big for its body. The *thing* let out a bloodcurdling sound that reminded me of a high-pitched tornado siren I'd heard during a trip to Oklahoma years prior. What unnerved me was the lack of mouth or nose. The malformed *thing* I interrupted was clearly not human which led me to wonder, *what exactly was I looking at? Could monsters actually be real?*

The thing made a sudden jittery movement as if it were planning to charge me. Startled, the flashlight slipped from my sweat-soaked palm as I tried to regain control of my body. It tumbled through the air before hitting the soft ground with a *thwap*. The flashlight landed in such a way that it centered the thing in its beam—resembling a deer caught in headlights. Its long skinny arms draped beside equally skinny legs. Grey, nearly translucent skin tightly wound around a skeletal frame not too different from my own. It moved out of sight with a cat-like agility.

I immediately lost track of where it fled as it scampered away into the field of tall grass.

Bending over to pick up my flashlight, I spotted what I'd hoped I wouldn't. Daphne was laying on her side in the grass staring straight at me with pained expression. Luckily, she was still alive so there may have been some hope of saving her, though I could see the agony in her eyes.

As I slowly approached her, I winced as the sight of her abdomen. It had been cut open with clean, almost surgical precision. The edges of the wound appeared to be cauterized, leaving no traces of blood on the open gash, though her exposed viscera hanging loosely from her gut was coated in blood. Pinkish amniotic fluid pooled around the ground near her belly and her uterus had been sliced open. Her piglets were nowhere in sight.

I knelt down, rubbing the spot between her ears I knew she liked, attempting to comfort her in her final moments. I called for my dad, the only thing I could think to do at that moment, but my voice sounded unusual. My calls were somehow chambered, as though resonating off an invisible wall, like I was in the shower and not the open air. I tried yelling again, but the echoes of my screams painfully reverberated in my head. I cupped my ears until the echoes stopped before giving up on my fruitless attempts for help.

My attention was drawn to the night sky, and I looked up to see the stars had vanished. Moments before, they were a prominent fixture, speckling the skyscape. Twinkling diamonds as far as the eye could see. Now they were gone. The darkest black I'd ever seen. Like the vast emptiness between the stars just opened up and swallowed the whole of my existence. I'd never felt so alone, yet I was only a few hundred yards from my house where my family sat watching the television.

Like a periscope breaching the surface of the dark sea, I stood up planning to escape back to the house—assuming I'd be able to run at all. My house was gone as was the barn. Despite my ignorance involving my current predicament, panic receded. An out-of-place feeling of calm swept over me. I welcomed the darkness as it devoured the fence I'd helped my dad build years ago.

I looked back at Daphne. My movements felt delayed, like an old-timey stop motion flick. Her deep breaths sent multicolored ripples into the air like pebbles dropped into a pond. I could feel her energy pulsing and somehow forging with my own. I moved my hand and observed the same ripple effect escaping my fingers, like my movements somehow manipulated the space around me. I tried to make my way down to join her on the ground but was met with nothing but cold empty space. I reached for her hoof, and we hovered there together in the dark. Stuck in limbo, in the space between wakefulness and sleep, when you're aware of your surroundings, but slowly drifting into a dream world. Voices and faces not part of your reality seep their way into your consciousness. Some are familiar, most are not. But not here. It was just me and my father's prized sow.

I peered into the depths of Daphne's eyes. They let me know she was not afraid, for she was now at peace. Despite the fact that her innards were spilling out, her pain and discomfort had seemingly diminished.

A warm, azure brilliance from above slowly bled into our surroundings until we were engulfed. My heart fluttered beyond nervous palpitations, but I remained irrationally still and unbothered. I looked to the source of the light—a rotating sphere flickering a mosaic of colors that made me think of a disco ball at the school dance. Returning my gaze outward, the light surrounding us was gone and we found ourselves floating in a star-filled expanse. Overlooking the curvature of the Earth, now miles below our feet, I tried to scream but no sound came.

Pulled skyward away from my home, I looked up. In awe of the sight before me, a massive saucer-shaped craft made of highly reflective chrome stretched out as far as the eye could see. So reflective, it was almost deemed invisible to the naked eye. I stared with a peculiar sense of dread, unwilling to take my eyes off of the sheer beauty of the object suspended above me.

I tightened my grip on Daphne's hoof as we drifted through an opening in the hull of the vessel. I didn't want to be alone, nor did I want her to be alone. The stars were gone; so was the Earth. *My home.*

Now inside the anomaly, Daphne and I were greeted by the familiar glow of what I thought were fluorescent lights. Our bodies remained still, paralyzed against our will. On the outer edges of the light, I could just make out silhouettes of dozens of figures moving towards us. Bizarre humanoid creatures that resembled the thing I saw outside the barn. Their heads tilted from side-to-side, a universal showing of curiosity.

I knew nothing was in my control. I began to panic. We were here to be observed. Poked and prodded like a science project. I had the feeling I was not meant to be there. I was an intruder. A stowaway that they were not expecting. Initially, I worried what they might do if they had no use for me, but I could feel the energy in the room was that of bemusement, not anger. My mind pondered what horrific experiments they might perform now that they had me in their control.

The figures kept their distance. I could feel their almond-shaped eyes curiously gazing over every inch of our bodies until one of them moved closer towards Daphne and myself.

I had no idea what to expect, but when the figure stepped into the light and revealed itself, I *knew* it was the thing I saw briefly by the pigpen. In my confusion, I'd almost forgotten I'd seen this thing in my yard.

Tonight? *Was that this evening*? I thought.

My memories were scattered as I tried to recollect everything that happened up to this moment, but it all seemed so distant. So long ago.

I had no idea how much time had passed. If I was being honest with myself, I could have passed through all of eternity, and it wouldn't have made any difference.

The being slid its fingers across Daphne's skin, looking her over methodically. It noticed my hand clutching her hoof and when it looked over at me, I could see it lacked expression. Still even in this close proximity under the bright lights, no mouth or nose. Just large, beaming eyes that were so dark, they might have contained whole universes inside and I would be none-the-wiser.

The being gently grabbed me by the wrist with its three long fingers and one stubby thumb. It pulled my hand, separating me from Daphne. I felt a rush of sadness as something inside me knew it would be the last time I would see my friend. I gazed into Daphne's large, round eyes and said goodbye.

My sadness was overshadowed by fear as I felt a hand cover the entirety of my face. It felt warm and clammy on my skin. The last thing I remember was a feeling of exhaustion before losing consciousness.

§

I opened my eyes. Stars twinkled above me, and I followed a shooting star as it shot across the canopy of space. My clothes were damp, and I was cold. My head felt swimmy, so I sat up slowly. The flashlight was lying next to me in the grass, shimmering brightly off the dew. I regained my composure, picked up the flashlight, and found my feet.

To my relief, the fence and the barn had returned. My heart sank as the light shone on the patch of matted grass where I'd found Daphne. She was gone, and I was in trouble.

The familiar voice of my mother called from the distance. I looked to the house, relieved it too had returned. The porch light revealed the Adirondack chairs, my mother's flower boxes, and the row of work boots we'd set out to dry. My mother's silhouette waiting for me on the front steps. Her hand bowed across her brow as she tried to see what I was doing on the outskirts of the pig pen.

Everything was seemingly back to normal. I could hear the muffled snorts of the herd in the barn settling down for the night.

Had I fallen asleep? Perhaps imagined the whole thing?

There was only one way to find out.

Shining the flashlight toward the house, I called back to my mother, telling her I'd be in momentarily. That's when two tall men stepped out from behind either side of her. She mumbled something to the men then pointed in my direction. They were dressed in expensive-looking black suits with matching fedoras, looking like characters in the old detective flicks my dad liked to watch. The strangest part of their attire was the sunglasses. They just stood there expressionless eyeing me suspiciously as my mother gabbed their ears off about my chores, raising a responsible boy, etc.

Breaking free of their hypnotic stares, I walked back to the barn and in through the open door. I rechecked all the pens and saw all the pigs snuggling each other in their designated corners. A few squinted as my intrusive flashlight disturbed their peaceful slumber.

I approached the final pen. At first, it appeared empty. Nothing but scattered hay.

It had all really happened, I thought.

The realization of my experience mixed with the fact that I would have to try to explain what had happened to my family's prize sow sent a surge of anxiety tearing through my body.

I started to turn and head out of the barn when something caught my eye. A rustling in the corner, under a small pile of hay. A tiny, newborn piglet wiggled its way out from beneath the bedding where Daphne had slept every night. The piglet looked around before it spotted me holding the flashlight. I didn't know what to think.

As my mind raced, wondering what this all meant, the piglet started towards me. When it reached the gate of the pen, it stuck it's tiny pink snout through the gap and snorted, as if to say, "hello".

I bent down to pet its head in the spot Daphne had often slept in, plucked a piece of straw off its snout, and laughed. No one would ever believe me.

I remembered thinking, *perhaps tomorrow I'll bring the little one a bite of chocolate.*

The only thing left that felt certain after that fateful night out at the pigpen, was I was no longer a skeptic.

§

"And that's everything I can remember."

The woman in the white lab coat scribbled a few more lines into her notepad, adjusted her glasses, and leaned back in her chair.

"Well, Mr. Branson, I appreciate your time and honesty. This will help our medical team immensely with the diagnostic process," she said, clicking her pen and setting it on the desk. "Your physical exam is scheduled for Thursday morning."

"Diagnosis? What are you talking about? I'm not making this up, lady. It really happened to—"

"Oh don't worry, Mr. Branson," the woman said in a calm voice. "We know you *believe* this really happened to you. Schizotypal personality disorder, while not all that common, is treatable under proper observation and medication."

"Schizo-what? Observation? What does all that mean?"

"We have no doubt you'll find our facilities quite exceptional." Her feigned smile did little to convince the young man sitting across the desk that she was being sincere.

The growing panic was evident as the young man began to shift in his chair.

"But...but...you can't just keep me here against—"

The woman ignored the pleas for mercy, pressed the call button on her telephone, and spoke aloud into the receiver in a more formal tone. "We're done in here. Please escort the patient back to his room."

The door opened behind the Mr. Branson. Two men wearing olive green scrubs and surgical masks walked to either side and gently helped him to his feet.

"I thought you said I was going home if I told you the truth. You can't keep me here!"

The men in green escorted the patient out the door and into the corridor. "I HAVE RIGHTS! STOP THIS NOW! *LET ME GO!*"

As the men in green led him down the corridor like cattle, the mocking chants of other patients reverberated off the concrete walls around them.

The woman in the lab coat let out a deep sigh, slipped the paperwork into a manila folder labeled **CONFIDENTIAL: PATIENT RECORDS**, then stood up from her desk. Walking to the window, she pulled open the blinds and peered down at a jet black luxury sedan that was parked in front of Greenfield Psychiatric Facility.

Down below, two pale-skinned men in fancy black suits and sunglasses stood on either side of the car. They looked up as the woman in the lab coat flashed them a thumbs up. Without a word, they opened the car doors, stepped inside, and disappeared behind the tinted windows.

The unmarked sedan lurched forward then sped off, sending a whirlwind of dead leaves and dust into the brisk, autumn air.

The blinds closed once more, and the woman sat back down at her desk. She lifted a manila folder from the intake basket, cleared her throat, then pushed down on the call button.

"Bring in the next patient."

TO FEAST WITH ORPHANS

The coils of garland twinkled beneath a dusting of snow on the light poles lining Main Street. All the patrons that bustled from shop to shop earlier that day were now at home nestled in their beds, or in front of a roaring fire. The shops—now closed—were lit from within, proudly displaying annual Christmas displays behind frosty storefront windows. A sight to behold, enough to send anyone out on a nighttime excursion for holiday spirit.

On the corner, a familiar sight for this time of year. A man dressed as Santa Claus stood beside a bright red suspended collection bucket. A single brass bell rang in time with the motion of his hand. No one was around to hear his bell, yet he continued to ring it.

Among whistling brisk winter winds, a chorus of slurred baritone carolers skittered along the icy sidewalks, rounding the corner of Fifth and Main. A trio of men—Jack, Todd, and Frank—unceremoniously dressed in flannel shirts, blue jeans, and matching red trucker hats stumbled onto Main. Out of place among the sights of the season, their bellicose banter and obnoxiously loud singing made it obvious they'd just departed the nearby pub.

A pack of wolves, eager to sniff out a few lonely she-wolves, they were disheartened to see Main Street was abandoned. The canopy of fresh snowfall covered any trace of the midday consumers.

Regardless of the holiday decor, Main Street had an eerie ambience to it. Things were too cheery. Too merry. Too perfect to be so *empty*.

The trio continued down the sidewalk, stumbling into each other, joshing about who was least likely to score a piece tonight. As they passed Hanscott's Handmade Fudge, they heard the jingling of a bell. Pausing to listen, they spotted a jolly old elf on the corner of Sixth and Main. Safeguarding a red bucket that hung from a tripod, the Santa Claus was ringing a heavy brass bell. The side of the bucket had the image of a pink heart with a smiley face painted onto it.

Jack—the presumed alpha—looked up and down the street for lingering eyes before turning back to his wolfpack with a sneer. They'd spotted vulnerable prey. It was time to encircle their kill and take what was—in their minds—rightfully theirs.

The bell reverberated between the facade of brick buildings as the Santa Claus paid no mind to the group of rough-looking men heading his way. Unexpectedly, the men initiated a chorus of, *Hark! The Herald Angels Sing.* Even more unexpectedly, they were in tune. Still, Santa remained indifferent to the carolers that fast approached his corner.

RING-RING RING-RING RING-RING

The men surrounded the street corner Santa, singing deafeningly into the old man's face.

RING-RING RING-RING RING-RING

When they finished their second chorus, Jack reached up and snatched the bell out of the Santa's white-gloved hand.

"That's enough of that noise, *Santa*," he said, mockingly, "can't you see all the people have gone home to their families?" His warm, whiskey-sour breath sent flecks of spittle onto the Santa's white beard. "Whatcha got in the bucket, old man?"

"These are collections for the children of the local orphanage. It's nothing for you gentlemen to be concerned about," the Santa replied.

Standing uncomfortably close behind him, Todd chimed in, "is that so?"

"I think we'll be the judge of that," Frank said, tipping the bucket for a better look inside.

"Don't touch that! I told you, that's not of your concern," the Santa said, sounding agitated, but not frightened by the random acts of aggression. "Give me back my bell," he demanded, holding out his gloved hand.

Jack grew red in the face. He and his pals were stronger, younger, and *clearly* a threat. The severe lack of concern on the old man's face angered Jack, whose whole shtick was fear-based dominance.

"Okay, sir. No problem. I can see that we're not welcome on *your* street corner." Jack's aggressive tone slightly diminished, but his hand white knuckling the varnished wooden handle of the bell was clearly an attempt to intimidate the old man.

As the Santa reached down to remove the invasive hand from his bucket of offerings, the brass bell came crashing down on the back of his head, splitting his scalp open with a spray of warm blood, sending his red, wool-lined hat down onto the snowy sidewalk. The Santa let out a gasp.

Caught off guard, he staggered backwards with a whimper, bumping into Todd who promptly locked him in a choke hold. Frank immediately started to empty the loose change and small bills from the collection bucket into his pockets.

Jack stepped in front of Todd to get a good look at the old man. "Ya know, it's a shame you didn't just give up the money. You might have lived to see Christmas morning."

The Santa, starting to get weak in the knees, stared back defiantly. He made a deep guttural noise like he was going to vomit, then spit out a sugar plum-sized loogie into Jack's face.

The other two bozos let out "Oooooohs," like they were kids in high school egging on the bully.

Jack was not so amused.

"Too bad you won't live to regret that, asshole." Jack pulled out a switchblade and snapped it open. The razor blade reflected the blue lights of Conroy's Bookstore. "Nah. That's too easy." He closed the blade and placed it into his back pocket. He looked down at the bell in his left hand and switched it to his right.

"Do it, Jack!" Todd egged him on.

"Yeah, you can't let him get away with that!" Frank jumped in.

The Santa, having regained some of his strength, stood up straight like he was going to make a move. Instead, he began to recite an old Christmas song.

"You better watch out, you better not cry, you better not pout, I'm telling you why. Santa—"

Jack raised the bell—*RING*—and brought it down with full force onto the old man's head with a loud crack. The already bloodied scalp tore further, leaving a flap of skin and hair hanging loosely from his exposed skull.

Todd's face was showered with blood. Frank belly laughed; his pockets jingled, stuffed full of the donations for the orphanage. The Santa gritted his teeth, then his mouth fell agape, and he let out one final exhalation.

Jack was not finished. Swinging the bell from the side—*RING*—he hit the old man in the temple, knocking him loose from Todd's chokehold.

The Santa dropped down onto the sidewalk, face planting in the snow without any resistance at all. Not moving. Not breathing. Jack kicked the old man in the rib but got no reaction.

"You killed the old bastard. He shoulda listened to ya, huh Jack?" Todd asked.

Jack chuckled, "This bell won't be no good anymore. He dented it all to shit with his head." Jack tossed it onto the ground beside the body.

"We'd better hold onto that, Jack," Frank said, picking up the bell to assess the damage, wiping off a chunk of hair and blood covered flesh, then tucking the bell into his back pocket. "Don't be needing them finding your fingerprints all over this thing considering you just got out of the slammer a week ago."

"Looks like the orphans won't be getting any presents this year," said Todd, amusedly.

Frank laughed, patting his pockets, making the change jingle again.

"Good. Fuck em!" Jack looked down, sucked in a wad of phlegm, and spit on the dead man. "Let's get out of here. We'll divvy up the money. We need to grab some beer before Quikmart closes."

The trio rounded the corner and headed down Sixth Street. Jack shot a glance back at the bloody scene and for the briefest moment felt a pang of guilt. Then as quickly as it came, it was gone.

Unbeknownst to them, a pair of eyes, cloaked in the darkness of Upper Sixth Street, watched as the men walked into the storm.

§

Sixth Street was the polar opposite of Main. It was dark and dreary, the winds seemed to have picked up their intensity, biting their skin through their thrift store flannel shirts, and the snow was getting deeper. Christmas was nowhere in sight on Sixth—besides the small Christmas tree that decorated the concrete steps of the Happy Hearts Orphanage. The windows were dark, and all was quiet.

Todd was the first to break the silence, "Jesus, Jack. Ain't that the orphanage the old man was going on about?"

"Of course it is."

"It's creepy. Where are all the kids?" Frank said, shivering with his arms clutching each other for warmth.

"Well, it is after midnight, Genius. You think maybe they're in bed?" Jack said, sounding annoyed.

"Fuck, it's freezing. How much further is the store?" Todd asked.

"Yeah man, screw the beer. I need something warm," Frank agreed.

"How about a nice cup of hot cocoa, boys?" A wispy disembodied voice proposed from between two buildings. Startled, the guys whipped around and squinted hard to see through the pitch blackness of the alleyway. Frank pulled the heavy bell from his back pocket and held it up in a defensive stance.

"Who's there?" Jack called. "Come out, now."

No response came from the dark. Just the whistling of the wind.

"Who said that?" Frank called next. "Fuck off!" he said, chucking the bell into the darkness.

Todd looked up and down the street to see if anyone was sneaking up on them. He paused at the sight before him. Pulling in an involuntary gasp, the bitter cold air burned his throat.

"Uhm...guys."

Jack and Frank both turned at the same time to look. Their faces lit by the light pouring out of the orphanage windows that appeared pitch black only a moment ago.

"Gentlemen—"

In their dismay, they hadn't noticed the man standing between the open double doors of the main entrance who was now calling to them.

"—you're liable to freeze to death if you don't get out of this storm. Please, won't you come inside and warm your bones? We won't take no for an answer."

Jack, Todd and Frank looked at each other with stunned expressions. Something definitely felt off about this, but the strange man was right. They wouldn't get far in this storm.

Todd was the first to accept the offer. Shrugging his shoulders, he started to cross the street and walk up the steep, snow-covered steps. Frank was next, almost giddy as he pounced in the snow, making his way up towards the man.

Jack hesitated. Looking back at the alleyway once more then back to the entrance of the orphanage. The shadows of his friends stretched out over the steps and across the street. Something about this didn't sit right with him.

Just as he was about to turn down the offer, he caught a whiff of something in the air.

Christmas cookies, he thought. A euphoric rush of nostalgia overwhelmed his senses, and without another thought, he followed in the path of his two friends.

"Atta boy, Jack. Come on in and make yourself at home," the man warmly greeted.

Jack looked up skeptically, curious as to how the man knew his name. *One of the guys must have said it. Yeah, that's it,* he erroneously convinced himself, then continued up the steps against his better judgement.

Once they were all in the building, they stood in the wide entryway, looking at their surroundings, shaking off the snow. Behind them, the man battled with the wind to close the heavy double doors. As they slammed shut, a familiar sounding bell chimed, and the man slid a heavy brass bolt across the door.

The man turned to get a better look at the guys and smiled. That's when

Jack spotted the clerical collar. He'd always felt uncomfortable around men of the cloth, ever since he was a child. The collar left him feeling unnerved, but he supposed it was a common sight at an orphanage.

The odor inside was much different than what Jack had smelled on the street. It was no longer the sweet aroma of Christmas cookies, but an equally pleasant feast of sorts. As pleasurable as the smell was, it was off-putting seeing as it was the middle of the night.

"So, gentlemen. Welcome to Happy Hearts Orphanage. I am Father Thibodeau. I maintain the operations of the orphanage through donations from the church collection basket as well as our team of volunteer Santas that graciously collect donations this time of year." He paused, eyeing the three men suspiciously, still wearing his holier-than-thou smile.

"Something smells delicious," said Todd, trying to change the subject and sniffing the air like a starving mongrel.

"Ah yes, you guys are just in time for dinner. We're having a special dinner to celebrate the arrival of the Yuletide," his voice sounded oddly whimsical. "We rarely have guests, so this will be an extra special occasion, especially for the children. They just love company."

"Well, we can't stay long, but we appreciate the offer. Just want to warm up a bit before we head back out and on our way," Jack said, sounding skittish. "I don't want my car getting towed."

"Oh pish tosh, you'll do no such thing until you've joined us for dinner. I insist. In fact—" Father Thibodeau sniffed at the air, "I believe it's almost ready!"

"Great!" Todd and Frank replied in spontaneous unison. Both were obviously hungry and not catching on to the fact that Jack didn't want to be there any longer.

"Oh splendid! That settles it," Father Thibodeau said, clapping his hands together. "Uh say, do either of you have any experience in the kitchen? One of our kitchen staff just up and quit recently. I'm sure Seymour could use a hand to finish up with the main course."

Frank raised his hand, "I do! I used to work in the kitchen at the jai—" he paused, "in the navy."

"Well this night just keeps on getting better and better. Please, gentlemen, if you'll follow me to the dining room, I'll show Frank here to our kitchen."

Frank, Todd and Father Thibodeau started down the hallway while Jack lagged behind.

How does this guy know our names? He thought, becoming more uneasy with the whole thing, before slowly following the group to the dining hall, mostly out of curiosity.

The dining hall was a large room with a high cathedral ceiling. A long rectangular shaped table in the center. It looked more like the dining hall of some medieval castle than that of an orphanage. All the high back chairs encircling the table were occupied by children, making them look enormous. Well, all but three. In the back of the room was a wide stone fireplace that looked like it could heat the whole building if it were lit.

"Please gentlemen, have a seat. I'll show Frank here to the kitchen. Dinner will be out momentarily," Father Thibodeau said, watching Jack and Todd as they walked towards the empty chairs at the far end of the table. The children also watched. "Oh, I almost forgot. Please leave the chair on the end open."

"Sure, no problem," Jack responded, finally breaking his momentary silence.

Jack and Todd sat across from each other, leaving the seat at the head of the table open as requested. Father Thibodeau proceeded to the kitchen with Frank following close behind.

"This is nice, huh?" Todd asked in a low voice.

Jack shot him a crooked smile, peering down the table. The children were all staring at the two guests with blank expressions of indifference. Todd looked down the table soon after, noticing something he hadn't before. The children all had uniformly white hair, deep blue eyes, with skin as pale as milk.

Todd looked back at Jack with a furrowed brow, mouthing the word 'okay,' at him.

Jack picked up on the other oddity that Todd had seemingly missed; the table hadn't been set. No plates, cups or silverware that would be customary for a feast.

The children continued to stare.

"Hi," Todd said, trying to ease the awkward tension. "Do you kids like it here?"

No response.

"Father Thibodeau seems nice."

Again, no response. Just uncomfortable stares.

"Must be shy," Todd whispered to Jack behind a discretionary cupped hand.

Jack and Todd sat patiently in the quiet room, hoping that dinner would arrive soon. Jack grew impatient as Todd twirled his thumbs.

Just as Jack went to say something to Todd, a noise came from the fireplace. A bit of debris and dust dropped from the chimney. Nothing too out of the ordinary considering it was storming outside, but then it happened again. This time it was followed by a scraping noise that steadily got louder, as if something was sliding down from above.

Suddenly, the children who hadn't made a peep began to clap and cheer, "Santa, Santa, Santa!"

Todd and Jack turned to look at the children, then back at each other, their hearts racing.

"Santa, Santa, Santa!"

They looked back at the fireplace, eyes wide as snowballs when a pair of scuffed black boots dropped down into the pile of ash below. Maybe a trick of the light, but Jack swore he saw a bone rise up from the ashes. Jack sat up straight, unsure of what was going on.

A hand in a white glove, blackened from soot, reached out and grabbed the outside of the fireplace, followed by a man in a red suit and hat. Pulling himself out of the fireplace, he stood up straight and looked directly at Jack and Todd. It looked just like the Santa Claus from the street corner. But it couldn't be. He was dead.

His skin was bluish grey as if he'd been frozen stiff. His lips were split, eyesblack as coal, and he had streaks of reddish-brown blood that had hardened and pooled onto the left side of his face.

He was dead alright.

Santa was wheezing heavily as he walked to the empty chair at the head of the table, never taking his eyes off Todd and Jack.

The children stopped chanting as soon as Santa sat down.

Jack was terrified and could hardly breathe. He wanted to stand up and run away, but he couldn't move. Todd seemed to be in the same state of paralysis.

Santa reached up and pulled off his red hat. It made a wet, peeling sound as it separated from the blood and brain matter of his head wound beneath. They could see pieces of scalp dangling loosely from the back of his head and the deep gash on his temple.

Jack swallowed hard, closed his eyes, and all the drinks he'd had at the pub earlier that evening released themselves into his blue jeans, running down onto the floor in a rush of warmth.

Breaking the tension, an awful sounding bell began to ring. Jack and Todd turned to see Father Thibodeau standing at the entrance of the dining hall swinging a bell at his side. A bell that was dented beyond repair.

"Children and our esteemed guests, dinner has finally arrived. We'll start with the main course then move onto dessert."

Father Thibodeau moved to the side to make way for a serving cart pushed by who the men assumed was Seymour. On the cart was a large stainless-steel cloche, like you'd see in a restaurant, only much bigger. They pushed the cart up to the table and carefully slid the cloche to the center. The children began to pound their fists in unison against the tabletop. The sudden disruption added to Jack and Todd's nervousness.

"Now, now, children. Let's settle down. Oh good! Santa has returned home just in time to eat! Jack, would you care to do the honors?" Father Thibodeau asked.

"Erm, not really. As I said before, I'm not hungry."

"Hmmm, well then, Todd. How about you? You look like you have quite the appetite."

Todd looked across at Jack, as if looking for approval. "Well, it does smell delicious. Why not?"

"Marvelous!" Father Thibodeau said, clapping his hands together.

Todd, freed of his temporary paralysis, stood up and walked to the center of the table. Squeezing in between two of the children, he reached over and pulled the heavy lid off the cloche. A cloud of steam rushed out from under the lid and the smell of cooked meat and veggies filled their senses. As the steam cleared, Todd and Jack saw what was on the platter.

Todd fell backwards onto the floor, dropping the lid with a loud metallic clang.

"Oh, Jesus Christ! *Frank*!" Jack pushed back off the table skidding his chair along the floor, anxiously looking about the room for the nearest exit.

Santa began to laugh loudly in his chair when he noticed Jack had pissed his pants. "HO-HO-HO-HOOOOO!" the last ho sounded more like a growl.

Frank was naked, kneeling and bent forward in the center of the platter. His skin was leathery and brown as if he'd been cooked. His eye sockets were hollowed out, hands were bound behind his back, and an apple had been shoved into his mouth. Enwreathed by a selection of green ruffage, steamed vegetables, and his own sauteed internal organs—he resembled a cooked hog.

"What the fuck did you do? What is this?" Jack stood from his chair.

"Why, it's our Yuletide feast, Jack." Father Thibodeau flashed him a devious smile. "Children, dinner is served!"

The children rushed from their chairs and leaped onto the table. They began ruthlessly ripping off chunks of Frank's flesh and muscle, devouring it with delight. Juices dripped from their chins as they tore through the meat with the razor-sharp teeth like wild animals.

"Oh fuck, oh fuck," Todd cried as he crab walked to the wall, pushing himself against it, shielding himself with the lid.

Father Thibodeau laughed and casually approached him. "Oh dear, Todd. There's nothing to worry about. The children only need to eat every so often. It's not every day their meal comes waltzing in from the cold. You could say Frank is providing a public service by feeding the needy."

"But he was our friend. You can't just—"

Smiling, Father Thibodeau slowly lowered the lid with his free hand as if to comfort Todd. Then he raised the brass bell above him and brought it down on Todd's head, knocking his trucker hat off onto the cold floor.

"...do that," Todd finished.

Two or three more hard hammer falls, and Todd collapsed to the floor in a pool of his own blood.

"*TODD!*" Jack went to make a run towards the door when several sets of little hands grabbed him and pinned him down into the chair. This caused Santa to laugh again.

"Get your hands off me! Let me go you *fucking monsters*!"

"Monsters? Tsk, tsk, tsk. I don't think you have any right calling my orphans monsters after what you did tonight, do you?" Father Thibodeau asked, approaching the head of the table carrying the freshly bloodied bell.

"It was an accident, I swear. I didn't mean to hurt anybody," Jack said, panicking and on the verge of tears. "Please, just let me go. I'm on parole. They'll come looking for me." He tried to muscle his way out of the grip of the children, but they were supernaturally strong. A few were licking him, starved for a second taste. The others were already on the ground, ripping Todd to pieces, devouring his raw meat.

"Bahaha! No one cares about garbage like you. We're doing society a favor. Are you not familiar with Matthew 5:38-42?" Father Thibodeau deepened his voice as if he were leading a sermon, "*Ye have heard that it hath been said, an eye for an eye, and a tooth for a tooth: But I say unto you, that ye resist not evil: but whosoever shall smite thee on thy right cheek, turn to him the other also*—I saw what you did this evening. Watched the whole thing."

"You're no holy man. You're just a bunch of cannibals. Filthy fucking animals."

Father Thibodeau shook his head as if disappointed, "I was really hoping this would go smoother." He turned to Santa, offering the bell, "Father Christmas, would you care to prepare the dessert?"

Santa grabbed the varnished handle of the bell and looked it over for a moment as if lost in the night's earlier events. Gradually standing up from his chair, he turned to Jack, appearing much bigger and more menacing than from his seated position. The children gripped him tighter. They dug their jagged claws into his flesh drawing blood and eagerly lapping it up like canines. Jack recoiled, his hand cupping his mouth.

Santa began to sing.

"You better watch out. You better not cry—"

"Please, don't do this! I'm so sorry," tears formed in Jack's eyes as he pleaded with the undead Santa.

"You better not pout—I'm telling you why."

He brought the bell down onto the center of Jack's skull, splitting it down the middle with a loud *crack*. The children let go and instantly tore Jack limb from limb. The snow-white hair of one child had been splattered with blood. Droplets pooled at the ends mirroring the dribbles that leaked from their mouths.

Santa stepped back and sat down at the head of the table to watch the orphans enjoy their annual Yuletide feast.

Father Thibodeau walked to the center of the table, reached down and pulled the apple from Frank's mouth. Frank's jaws remained agape as his body was picked clean by the children. Father Thibodeau sat in one of the chairs and took a bite of the apple, and he too watched as the children enjoyed their three-course meal.

"*Bless this food to our bodies, Lord, and let us hold you in our hearts. Merry Christmas to all God's children. In Jesus' name, we pray.*"

The children all looked up from their feast and replied:

Amen.

COMA TOAST

B ring it in here, fellas."

"Right here?"

"Yeah, open up that door. I believe there's an empty one in there."

"You got it."

A pop releases pressure, then there's rubbing of heavy hinges.

"Yep. Sure is."

"Great, load it onto that for me, would ya? I'll take it from there."

Squeaky wheels roll along a polished cement floor, a bump follows.

A sudden feeling of weightlessness then another bump.

"Here ya are, Tom. Can we do anything else for ya?"

"No, I should be all set. This one is straightforward. Barnes should be back shortly, at least I hope."

"You got it! Have yourself a nice weekend, Tom!"

"You too fellas. Don't stay out too late hitting the sauce."

Footsteps. A heavy metallic door slams shut. Clicking of a keyboard across the room.

"Eehhh... Come on, Barnes. I got shit to do, man."

The plastic wheels of a chair roll a short distance. A printer activates and prints a document, then stops. Papers shuffles. A stapler is punched. A phone rings and buzzes.

"Ugh, *Barnes*... Hello?"

Talking on the other end.

"You gotta be kidding me? It's Friday night, man. We got another one to—"

Talking on the other end.

"I know you can't control traffic, but *you* know I have a bad back... Yeah. They just dropped it off."

Talking on the other end.

"Of course it can't wait. We have orders to get it done tonight."

Talking on the other end.

"No, I can*not* wait an hour, man. I have dinner plans with my wife. It took us months to get these reservations."

Talking on the other end.

"Well that's simply perfect. Fuck my back, right, Howard? I'll just have to take care of it myself."

Talking on the other end.

"Well it'll be taken care of by the time you get back here. I'll be sure to leave the mess for you to clean up."

Talking on the other end abruptly cuts off.

"Bye, Howard!"

Receiver is slammed down.

"What an asshole! He pulls this shit all the damn time. Traffic, my ass!"

Chair wheels roll again, and fingers aggressively tap a keyboard.

"Well, let's get this thing fired up."

Footsteps echo across the room.

A loud click sounds.

Another click.

Footsteps approach.

Heavy, irritable sighs.

A long zipper is opened.

Coolness on my skin.

A bumping.

A pair of warm, clammy hands pull.

Grunting.

Audible breaths.

A cold metallic surface slides under my back.

"*Phew…* You're fucking lucky, Barnes. My wife would have kicked my ass if I showed up to dinner with another blown out back."

A metallic door slides open.

A blast of heat on my scalp and shoulders.

"I better get lucky tonight after how much I'm spending on this fucking dinner."

Metallic wheels roll beneath. Heat intensifies.

"In ya go. Barnes will be by to clean up your mess."

Heat envelopes my naked body.

"Fare thee well and good riddance!"

The metallic door shuts at my feet.

Body hair singes, and my skin melts like candle wax.

The smell of my flesh being incinerated permeates the cramped space.

The pain is too much but it's impossible to do anything about it.

Internal screams echo inside my head…

Tom watches the thermostat of the crematory reach 2200 degrees Fahrenheit. He nods his head in satisfaction, then steps outside to smoke a few butts.

An hour or so later, Tom walks back into the room looking at his watch.

"Couple of minutes left. Barnes is lucky I take this job more seriously than he does. Even luckier that I trust him as much as I trust a fart in church."

Tom finishes picking up the mess around the morgue. Sprays and wipes down the metal gurney and places it back into the cooler. Finally, he disposes of the body bag.

"That's good enough. Barnes can handle the rest. I have an anniversary to attend to."

Tom walks back to the desk. He picks up the paperwork to file it away when something catches his eye on the orders:

§

ATTN: To Be Delivered to Burnchester General ICU

Patient suffering from full body paralysis following a car crash that took place earlier this evening. Heavily sedated. Several broken bones incl. three in the cervical spine. Unable to speak or move limbs. Breathing slowly—possible coma.

Wife and two children who were also in the vehicle are fine; at the hospital being checked over. They'll meet patient there this evening once cleared by an ER nurse.

Please check in with RN on duty. Doctor Thurston will be by on Monday to check on patient. Full to partial recovery expected.

NOTE: *This man got lucky. Shouldn't have survived impact.*

§

Tom's labored breathing is cut short by the ringing of the telephone.
"H—Hello?"
"Yo, Tom! It's John. We fucked up big time, man! We bagged up the wrong guy. Huge mistake, right? Hehe. We're on our way with the body. We'll take that one to the ICU and switch it with the stiff. The death certificate should be in the printer any minute. Luckily the guy in the back had no family. I'm sure they'd be pretty pissed off. Sorry for the mix-up, man."
Tom stands there, numb. The telephone receiver is pressed firmly against his ear. His knuckles turn white from the tight grip, nearly crushing the plastic. Sweat gathers on his brow.
"Tom? You there, man?"
"Uhm... Yeah..." Tom turns. Eyes wide as he stares at the furnace. The clean metal gleams under the glow of incandescent tubes above.
"Tom, what's up? Did you hear me? Hello? We're on our way."
Tom slowly lowers the receiver returning it to the base. He lets himself fall back into the desk chair defeated. The wheels glide and the back of the

chair bangs into the desk shaking the cup of pens. He stares at the furnace. An audible *ding* (which always reminds him of his toaster oven at home) chimes alerting him that the job is done.

The goose is cooked, and it's well done.

Deafening silence follows. Tom hears the steady pounding of his heartbeat pulsate throughout his entire body. The back of his eyes drum with sharp pains from the oncoming migraine. The face of the man he murdered and burned alive forever etches into the back of his mind. His racing thoughts shift to the possibility of legal consequences for his error.

The man had a wife and two kids, he thought.

A cell phone chimes and buzzes on the desktop beside him, seemingly miles away. Hazily, Tom turns and reads the text message from his wife through bloodshot eyes:

I can't wait for dinner tonight!! Are you leaving soon? See you at the house.

PS - I hope you were planning on getting lucky tonight! ;)

A ROOM FULL OF TOYS

December 20, 1950

All of the party planning had come to fruition. Cocktails, caviar, cigarettes, fondu, the works. Several local bigwigs from the most prestigious law firm in town could be seen indulging in the hors d'oeuvres that had been prepared and arranged with the utmost care.

Mister Robichaud, the owner of the largest credit union in town, was fraternizing with his underage mistress. Mayor Prescott was conversing with Father Dunn from Saint Joseph's Catholic Church who was making a rare appearance. Even the governor was rumored to be showing his face. The party was bustling.

The house was enormous, yet nearly every room was filled with at least a handful of local socialites. All of them discussing sports scores, the latest gossip, sex scandals involving the young couple in the next room, politics, budgets, and the occasional novel.

Most of the guests were personally invited by the homeowners, Cordelia and Harold Crenshaw. Some had found themselves politely invited by an acquaintance in passing. And some were invited out of spite.

Such is the case with Rosemary Barbano and her two children, Jimmy and Bess. Rosemary worked at the local laundromat and regularly pressed Mayor Prescott's three-piece suit that he was so proud of. Prescott had caught wind of a potential challenge for his position as mayor by Harold, so being the conniving bastard he was, he thought it would be interesting to invite someone who *was not* part of the upper echelon of small town social structure. In other words, he was hoping to sabotage the party.

Rosemary sat on a loveseat in one of the living rooms wearing the nicest dress she owned. A tall handsome man named Greg approached and sat down beside her before introducing himself. Unbeknownst to him, Jimmy and Bess were both hiding under the loveseat exchanging pinches.

As the tall man leaned in to work his charm on Rosemary, Jimmy reached out from under the loveseat and pinched him hard on the ankle. Bess covered her mouth to hold in her laugh as Gregory let out a howl of pain.

"What in Jesus' name?" he called as he stood up and moved away from the loveseat.

The kids couldn't contain themselves and they both started laughing hysterically at their prank. Rosemary was less than amused.

"I'm so sorry. KIDS! You come out from under there this instant," Rosemary ordered. The children did as they were told, "you apologize to the nice man right now."

"We're sorry," they said in unison, with hardly any conviction.

"What are your kids doing here? This is a party for adults," Greg said, sounding appalled.

Rosemary looked embarrassed. "They said they were sorry. They're good kids. They didn't mean any harm."

"Yeah, well this is no place for children. Perhaps you shou—"

"What is going on in here?" Greg was cut off as Cordelia came into the room to see what the fuss was about.

"These little shits thought it would be funny to bite me in the leg," Greg scoffed.

Rosemary was taken aback by such a blatant lie. She wouldn't just stand here and listen to this man tell fibs about her children. "That's not what happened at all. The kids were just having a little fun. They get protective of their mother sometimes. Besides, they apologized."

"Okay. Okay. Miss...?"

"Barbano. Rosemary Barbano."

"Miss Barbano, if you would kindly take your children to the second floor. There is a room up there where they can play. Then you can come back down and introduce yourself further. Eh, first room on the right. I'll escort Mr. Herman here to the cocktail bar. I'm sure it's nothing a few martinis couldn't fix."

Rosemary thanked Cordelia then shot Gregory a scowl as she put an arm around each child to lead them to the playroom on the second floor.

She could just hear the man telling Cordelia, "she's lucky I don't sue her ass," as they left the living room.

"Kids, I appreciate you looking out for me, but how is Momma supposed to find anyone if you always sabotage things?"

They began to ascend the narrow stairway and each step let out an obnoxious *creak* underneath their feet.

"But Momma, that guy was a dingus," Bess said.

"Yeah, what a jerk. I should have pinched him harder. What a baby," Jimmy said.

Creak... Creak...

"Well, you may have just saved me a ton of headaches. I forgive you this time, but I'm still young. I don't want to be alone forever."

Creak... Creak...

They continued up the stairs.

"We know Momma, it would be cool to have a dad," Bess agreed.

"Well your dad was the most wonderful man. I just wish you two could have met him. He loved you both so very much and wanted more than anything to come home so he could meet you."

"What did you say his job was in the army?" Jimmy asked. He knew the answer, but it filled him with pride to hear his mother tell the story.

"He was a squad leader. Fought in the second world war. He lost his life just after you two were born. I know he would have loved to play with you. He was a big kid at heart."

"I'm sorry Momma, we won't mess up again. Promise. We don't want you to be lonely anymore," Jimmy said, feeling as much guilt as his ten-year-old body would permit.

"Yeah, Momma. We're sorry," Bess apologized.

Creak... Creak...

"It's okay, kiddos. Right now, I feel like the luckiest mother on Earth. I mean, look where we are. In the nicest house in town, socializing with the local elite. I have a steady job. We're all healthy," she said as they reached the second story landing, rounding the banister. The hallway was dimly lit and hardly welcoming. It was obvious that the hosts weren't expecting guests to bring their children. The air on the second floor was cooler and smelled musty. Rosemary assumed the owner's must spend most of their time on the first floor. She couldn't for the life of her understand why two people needed a house so big in the first place.

"We have to stay up here, Momma?"

"Just for a little while, Bess. I'm trying to make some friends in this town. It's not easy when I am constantly working at the laundromat. Mayor Prescott was nice enough to invite us and I didn't want to be rude and say no."

"It's fine, Bess. Look!"

Jimmy said as Rosemary pushed open the door to the playroom. Toys were scattered all over the room. Rocking horses, trains, jacks, clowns, Lincoln Logs, dolls, a chest filled with dress up clothing, a chalkboard, the works!

"WOW!" Bess exclaimed. Her eyes were aglow with amazement upon seeing the vast assortment of toys before her. They'd never seen so many toys.

"Can we live here?"

Rosemary laughed at Jimmy's question. "Sure honey. I bet they'd never even notice if you just hid inside that fancy old treasure chest in the corner."

"Why do they have so many toys if they don't even have any children?" Bess asked, always the inquisitive one.

"You know, that's a great question. Maybe they're collectors? I honestly don't know, kiddo. But you two play in here and behave for Momma. I'll be back up to collect you in an hour or so."

"Okay, Momma," they replied simultaneously. They weren't twins, Bess was the older of the two by over a year, but one might guess that they were by the way they acted.

As they ran to explore the toys, Rosemary slipped out of sight and returned downstairs to the party. She hoped she wouldn't come across Mister Herman again and knew in such a large home, the odds were in her favor.

Upstairs, the children had the time of their lives. Jimmy worked on constructing a castle using the largest collection of Lincoln Logs he'd ever seen. Bess brushed the hair of an adorable doll she'd found while rocking back and forth on a unicorn.

"Don'tcha think her hair looks good enough?"

"It was all knotted up! She's beautiful and deserves to be treated better than that. Why would they collect all these toys if they don't even take care of them?"

"I don't know, and I don't care. Hey, do you think they'd notice if I snagged a few of these log pieces?"

"How should I know?"

"I don't have any of these long pieces."

"Whoa, look! A record player!" Bess climbed off the rocking horse and sat the doll on the wooden seat. "Let's put on some tunes."

She walked towards the record player and stepped on something that poked her heel. A small plastic arm laid on the floor. She hadn't noticed any of the dolls missing an arm, so she tucked it behind her ear in case she came across one.

There was already a record on the turntable. She lifted the needle, gently swiveled it over, and lowered it onto the grooves—just like her mother had shown her in the listening room at the local library. The turntable began to spin.

A few crackles then Bing Crosby's smooth voice began to croon out from the speakers.

"Turn it up, Bess."

She didn't argue. She turned it so the knob was halfway to full volume.

The music lightened the mood in the toy room, no longer feeling so inhospitable.

"I wonder what kind of music Daddy liked. You ever wonder about that, Jimmy?"

"Sometimes. I bet he was a jazz man."

"What makes you think that?"

"I don't know, really... Just seems like something he would have—"

Thump-Thump.

"Whoa... did you hear something?" Bess asked.

"Yea, maybe it was just the party. Mom said they're having adult drinks down there, whatever that means."

Thump-Thump-Thump.

"There it is again! That was definitely from above us, Jimmy."

"Well maybe they have really big mice up there. Who knows?"

"You think so? Let's go check it out!" Bess said, always the adventurous one.

"We don't even know how to get up there. Besides, what if it's dark? We have no flashlight."

"Oh yeah?" Bess said, walking over to the toy chest and reaching in. "What d'ya call this then?"

Jimmy looked less than enthused. He was a bit of a scaredy cat and didn't feel like going crawling around in some dusty old attic.

"Can't we just stay here and play until Momma comes back? She said she would only be an hour or so."

"Come on you big baby! Don't be such a little giiiirl!" Bess coaxed.

"I'm no stinky girl! I just want to finish my castle."

"Suit yourself, Jimmy the Wuss. I'll go by myself then."

Bess started towards the door and clicked on the flashlight to test it out. Jimmy watched her walk into the hallway and disappear from sight. With him being alone in the room surrounded by toys, the music gave off an ominous presence and was no longer welcoming.

Thump-Thump-Thump.

That was enough for Jimmy. He jumped to his feet and bolted out of the toy room.

"Bess! Wait for me!"

She was waiting for him at the bottom of the second staircase that led up to the attic.

"I knew you'd change your mind," she said, trying hard not to tease him too badly, although she wanted to.

They could hear the bustle of the party still in full swing, so they assumed they had plenty of time to explore. Bess shined the flashlight up the stairs and saw where they came to an end.

"Let's go, Jenny."

"It's Jimmy, you jerk. D'ya want me to come or not?"

Bess laughed, "alright, alright. Don't get your skivvies in a knot. Let's go."

They started up the stairs and each step was accompanied by the familiar *creak* from the first stairwell. The music from the toy room and the party slowly faded as they reached a small landing that was only big enough to swing open the attic door.

"Okay, Brother. This is it. Stay behind me and hang onto my shirt. And watch your step. You don't want to step in any mouse poop. Mom would definitely know we were up to something then."

"Don't worry, I won't. I just wish I had my own flashlight."

"Alright, here we go," Bess said, sounding as though she were leading an expedition into some unexplored cave. She lifted the cast iron latch that held the attic door shut, releasing the pressure on the door it swung open all on its own.

"Well that was creepy," Jimmy said softly, with a twitch of nervousness in his voice.

"God, you're such a chicken. Are you sure we're related?"

Jimmy pinched Bess on her elbow. She resisted slapping him upside the head and pulled the door open enough so they could see into the attic.

A musty smell overwhelmed them along with something else they couldn't quite pinpoint. A cold draft whizzed through the door and slid across their exposed skin. They both felt a rush of goosebumps crawl over their flesh.

"I want my jacket," Jimmy said.

"Seriously? Toughen up. We've made it this far. Let's keep going."

They stepped into the attic and were thankful to see there was a sturdy floor and a high ceiling. This was quite different from other attics they'd explored in the past. Bess shined the light around the room and could see two chimneys rising up from the floor and through the roof. On either end of the room were big windows. One was octagon shaped and was facing

Pleasant Street where their mother had parked her car. The other was smaller, rectangular and looked out across the rooftops.

"We must be up so high!" Jimmy said, sounding more excited than scared.

"I didn't notice how big this house was when we got here since it was already dark."

"If it were daytime, bet we could touch the clouds just outside that window," Jimmy said.

"Don't be a dummy," her words were accompanied by warm puffs of vapor.

Chugga-chugga-chugga.

The sound coming from the far corner of the room interrupted their banter. They both stopped and didn't say a word. Something let out a mournful moan from the darkness.

"Did you hear that?" Jimmy asked, fear returning to his tone.

"Of course I did, I'm not deaf," Bess whispered.

"Come on, Bess. Let's just go back downstairs. Please!"

"No! I want to see what it is!"

She shined the flashlight across the floor checking for obstacles.

"There. Let's go but stay quiet. Whatever it is, I don't want it to hear us coming," Bess ordered.

Jimmy tightened his grip on Bess' shirt and walked as close as he could to her without stepping on her heels. He kept his eyes shut tight as Bess led the way. Halfway into the room they heard another *chugga-chugga-chugga,* followed by more moaning. Bess shined the light up off the floor and could just make out what looked to be a small closet that was built into the attic. She could see a door that was fashioned with a sliding lock near the top.

"That must be where the noise came from," Bess whispered.

Jimmy didn't reply, still holding on tight to his big sister's shirt.

"God, what's that smell? *Pee-yew!*"

Bess cupped her free hand over her nose. She traced the room with the beam of light and continued her approach. They could barely hear the sounds of the music from the toy room below.

"He-hello?" she called to the thing in the closet. "Is someone in there?"

"Hurro! Hurro!" a voice called back.

Bess gasped and turned to look at Jimmy who opened his eyes when he registered the sound of a new voice echoing his sister.

They walked up to the door and Bess set her ear against it.

"Hurro? Bing! Bing!"

Bess and Jimmy exchanged confused glances through the upward beam of the flashlight.

"Hold on. If you promise you're not dangerous, I'll open the door."

"Bing!"

"Don't do it, Bess. There could be anything in there!" Jimmy pleaded.

Ignoring him, Bess slid back the lock and pulled open the door. They heard a scuffling noise as the revolting stench of feces and urine blasted them both in the faces. Fighting the urge to vomit, Bess shined the flashlight into the room. To her surprise, the walls were covered in wallpaper with images of flower bouquets repeated from top to bottom. It was something you'd expect to see in a dining room. On the wall hung an eerie picture of a gnome that resembled Santa Claus wearing a red hat and green overcoat, feeding birds by hand in the snow. An octagonal window on the far side of the room overlooked the stillness of Pleasant Street.

On the floor laid an array of toys and pieces of toys, as if they'd been carelessly tossed in there. She shined their light into the far corner and gasped at what she saw. A child, no more than eight or nine years old, crouched down in the corner, attempting to hide their face in a kneeling fetal position. In front of them sat a small tin bucket.

Bess and Jimmy exchanged looks. Both were disturbed, but curious. This was not what they were expecting to find. Their young minds could hardly make sense of what was in front of them.

The child slowly peered out from between their knees, and the siblings could see what appeared to be a little boy. He was shivering, his skin was pale and chapped with raw red creases on his elbows and knees. His face was malformed in a way neither Bess nor Jimmy had ever seen before.

"Hi, I'm Bess. This is my brother, Jimmy."

The boy suddenly seemed less apprehensive, like he was happy to see the two young kids.

"What are you doing in there?" Jimmy asked, "do you live here?"

When the boy didn't respond, Bess decided to shine the light up to their faces so he could see what they looked like. "We aren't here to hurt you. We could hear you banging from downstairs. You know, the one filled with toys?"

The boy's face lit up with unexpected delight. "Bing! Bing!" the boy repeated, excitedly.

"Bing? What's he mean by bing?" Jimmy asked.

They could tell there was something different about him, but he seemed nice enough. Bess decided to take a chance and stepped into the tiny closet-sized room just inside the door, careful to keep from shining the light into the boy's eyes.

"What is bing? Is that your name?" she asked.

The boy smirked shyly and let out a goofy laugh as he forcefully shook his head.

He turned the rest of the way to face them and tapped his free hand on the floor and began to hum a melody.

Jimmy recognized it right away as the song from the record player they'd heard prior to coming up.

"What was the name on that record, Bess?" he asked her.

"Oh come on, Jimmy, everyone knows Bi..." suddenly it dawned on her. "*Bing!* Bing Crosby! Are you talking about Bing Crosby?"

The boy, still crouched, bounced up and down shouting, "Bing, Bing!" over and over again. Smiling, Bess turned to Jimmy, seemingly proud of herself for solving the mystery.

As she'd turned her head, the boy gasped and jumped up with an arm outstretched as if to grab her by the neck.

"Bess!" Jimmy called.

Before she could react, the boy snatched the doll arm from behind her ear. She fell back against the wall with the window and shined the light at him as if trying to deflect an attack.

He held the arm up to his face and stared in amazement. Turning it around to examine it from every angle. He leaped back into the corner and from the darkness pulled out a plastic doll. The boy held it up towards the light and they could see his doll was missing an arm.

He slid the arm he'd taken from Bess into the small hole. It was a perfect fit. A beaming smile ran across his face as he hugged the doll tightly against his collar bone. Despite his yellow cracked teeth, the smile was charming.

Bess took the moment of distraction to aim the light down into the tin bucket. It was filled with dark brown liquid and chunks of feces floating around. Startled, she dropped the flashlight and stepped out of the room to take in a breath of musty attic air. It smelled like a field of lavender compared to the confines of that tiny prison.

"Bess, are you okay? What is it?" Jimmy asked as he bent down to retrieve the flashlight.

"I'm okay, I just needed some air," she said. "I don't like tight spaces."

"What do you think he's doing in here?"

"Isn't it obvious, dummy? He's locked away up here in the attic, in the dark, with a tin to crap and pee in. It must have been his parents." She took back the flashlight and traced the beam around the tiny room.

"But why would they do such a thing?"

"How should I kn—" she started but was cut off by the boy.

"Pa-parents bad! Pa-parents put me here. I cold. I cold," he explained.

"Your parents? You mean Cordelia and Harold? But—why?" Bess asked.

"Pa-party. Pa-party."

"The party? Jeez Louise! That makes no sense," she said, sounding flabbergasted.

"I don't like this, Bess. I don't think we're supposed to be up here. We could get into serious trouble. Or worse, get Momma in trouble," Jimmy said.

"Well, we can't just leave him—err what's your name?"

The boy replied by shaking his head.

"What do you mean? You don't even have a name?"

He shook his head again.

"Jimmy, it's freezing up here. We can't just leave him alone like this."

"But I don't want to get in trouble! I just want to go back to the toy room and play until Momma comes back. For all we know, she's looking for us right now," he pleaded. His voice was heavy with desperation.

"Don't be such a baby!"

At this, the boy hugged his doll again and tears began to roll down his cheek, clearing away a sliver of dirt with their trail.

Bess snatched the flashlight from Jimmy's hand and shined it at the boy. "What should we do? Do you want to come out of here and go down to the toy room with us? If you stay up here all night, you'll freeze to death!" Bess warned.

The boy shook his head forcefully from side-to-side and backed away into the corner. Fully visible for the first time, Bess took in the boy's bruises. The flesh on his arms and legs had been covered with swollen purple spots and deep scratches. His wrists and ankles were enwreathed with dark rings as if he'd been wearing handcuffs or shackles.

"What's wrong? Don't you want out of this awful place? Maybe we can find you some help. Our mom can take you to a doctor," she continued. "She's a really nice lady."

The boy let out a deep, sorrowful moan and tucked his body as far as he could into the corner, still hugging his doll.

"Bess, we're just kids. We don't know the whole story. He could be dangerous. I just don't want to get in trouble. Momma is finally making friends." She knew his heart was in the right place, but she also knew she'd never be able to live with herself if she left this boy up here in this dark room.

"I don't know. Won't you please come with us?" She pleaded with the boy. He just crouched into the corner, ignoring her question. "Please! Come with us, we'll get you help!"

When he gave no response, Jimmy was ready to go.

"Bess, he doesn't want to come. Just leave him alone and we'll act like we never saw anything. We'll go back downstairs and wait for Momma to come get us like we planned all along."

She stared longingly at the boy for a moment, a solitary tear trickling down her pale cheek.

"Please..."

When he would not respond, she decided it was time to give up. Her heart ached at her failed attempt to get him help. A tinge of anger flared up in her chest over how cowardly her brother was behaving. She knew she'd never be able to forgive her brother, nor would she forget the face of the boy that was too scared to leave the dark room in the attic for fear of what was in the light.

Looking up at the picture on the wall, the gnome-like man seemed more malevolent than she'd previously thought. The idea of this boy being locked in an unlit closet, with a few broken toys and a bucket to relieve himself while the man in the painting enjoyed his freedom and feeding birds out of his hand in the snow seemed cruel. Maybe the boy didn't see it that way though. The picture could represent an escape for him from his wretched confinement. A happier place where he could go in his mind when the light seeped in through the window. With that thought, the face seemed more happy than evil. The gnome-like man seemed at peace. A peace the boy may never truly find outside of the frame of the painting.

Bess gave up. She was ready to call it quits. There were no words she could say that would change this boy's mind. As painful as it was, she would have to accept that.

"I won't ever forget you. I'll come back for you, one day. I promise."

"Bess, come on," Jimmy said, tugging on her forearm, halfway out the door.

"I promise," she said before stepping back into the attic, closing the door, and sliding the lock into place.

Noticing Jimmy had already made his way back to the stairwell, she paused outside the door. Turning the corner of the tiny closet, she peeked inside the window one last time and shined the flashlight in.

The painting smiled at her, the beam reflected off the side of the tin bucket, and the boy looked up from his crouched fetal position. His cheeks were wet with tears and his hand stroked the long blonde hair of the doll he held lovingly in his bruised hands. He looked up at her one final time as if to say goodbye, but his eyes said more than that; they said *thank you.*

She waved to him, placed her hand against the ice-cold pane of glass, then joined her brother at the doorway. The distant sound of Bing Crosby could be heard from down below. Even more distant were the sounds of chattering adults and boring chamber music coming from the party.

"Come on, sis. Let's go wait for Momma," Jimmy said, sounding thankful.

He placed a hand on his sister's shoulder which she immediately swatted away before she walked past him and retreated down the stairs.

Suddenly realizing he was standing in the doorway of the dark attic all alone, he quickly stepped onto the landing and slammed the door shut, being sure the latch caught on the hook.

Back in the playroom, Jimmy returned to constructing his castle of Lincoln Logs without a care in the world. Bess sat amongst the dolls that were displayed below a large picture window that overlooked the side yard. She remained there, quietly stroking the hair of one of the dolls, listening to the needle on the record skipping after the last song was over.

"Hey kiddos!" Rosemary greeted them as she walked into the room full of toys.

"Hey Momma!" Jimmy said, overly enthusiastic. "Come check out my castle! Isn't it great?"

"Wow, buddy! That's amazing! Maybe you'll be a famous architect one day?"

"Think so?"

"Ya never know. You could even design beautiful houses for rich folks like this one someday," Rosemary encouraged.

"This house is *not* beautiful. It's evil," Bess spoke up, sounding agitated. "Can we *please* go home now? I never want to see this house again."

"Of course, my love," Rosemary said, her expression showing concern. "You guys didn't have fun? This room is full of toys! I would think it would be every kid's dream!"

"Well it wasn't. I just want to go home," Bess said, on the verge of tears.

"Okay, sweetheart, we can go. Thank you both for behaving tonight. Mr Hansen left shortly after I brought you both up here." She put an arm around Jimmy's shoulder and began escorting him out of the room.

"That's good, Momma. Did you make any friends tonight?" asked Jimmy.

"Well... I think so—"

"I'll be right down, Momma. I just need to do something before we go. I'll be right behind you guys."

"Sure thing, my love. Take your time," she said, leaving the room with Jimmy under her arm.

56

Bess gently set the doll back where she'd found it amongst the other dolls. She walked over to the record player, lifted the needle, and set it back down on the first track of the record. Next, she turned the knob to full volume and a melancholy ensemble of strings played out through the speakers, followed soon by Bing Crosby's soothing voice.

Bess smiled, looked up at the ceiling and quietly spoke one word to herself before leaving the room and joining her family downstairs.

"Bing."

§

December 23, 1998

The wipers struggled to keep up with the heavy snowfall. Bess watched out the window at the barely visible homes passing by but hadn't realized that they'd turned onto Pleasant Street. She'd been invited to her nephew's new home that he'd recently purchased to renovate and flip. After his father James passed away last year, he'd collected his inheritance and returned to his hometown to start buying up old properties.

As they got closer, a heavy, inexplicable feeling of dread washed over Bess and she considered asking her daughter to pull over so she could get some air. Ultimately deciding against it, she rolled down her window a notch instead.

She closed her eyes and took in a deep breath of the bitterly cold air. It felt good.

"Well Ma, we're here," Sarah said.

"Oh good, I was starting to get a little car sick."

"Oh no, was my driving that bad?" Sarah joked.

"No, no. It's the weirdest thing. When we pulled onto this street, I started to feel—" she stopped as she noticed the tall white pillars of the front porch. She recognized those pillars, and fancy lights that illuminated them.

"What street did you say we were on, dear?"

"Pleasant Street. Ma, your memory is getting worse by the day," Sarah said as she pulled into the driveway. "Remember? Tim's Christmas party?"

Vintage Christmas decorations lit up the side porch and the windows were brightly lit through the heavy snow.

A memory from the distant past flashed into her mind and goosebumps covered her thinning flesh. *Bing.* "No...Not this house," Bess said, almost on the verge of tears. *Bing.* "We cannot go in there."

"Ma, what's the matter? Tim's been working so hard to fix the place up. He will be heartbroken if you don't come in. We don't need to stay long."

"I know this house. I've been here before. A long time ago. I really don't want to go back there."

Bing! Bing!

Sarah looked at her mother, her concern clearly evident under the glow of the dashboard. "Well what happened? How come you've never said anything to me about it?"

Bess' eyes peered up through the windshield, seemingly trying to see up to the second floor. Flooded with memories of her and Jimmy hiding under the loveseat; her mother, so full of youth and beauty, the crackle of the record player and chatter of partygoers—the room full of toys. The memory was more like a ghost now. A spectral haunting the furthest reaches of her mind. Her memory may be slipping, but some things a person couldn't forget.

Bing!

"—Mom!" her thoughts were cut off by her daughter's abruptness. "Come on. It'll be alright. We don't have to stay long."

Hesitantly, Bess agreed and stepped out into the snow.

§

The party was bustling. Drinks, music, cheese and crackers, meats, the works. An album of Christmas tunes was in rotation on the CD player. Tim greeted them both as they walked through the door. It had been years since Bess last saw him and he was the spitting image of his father, Jimmy. Seeing Tim hurt her heart a little, but it was good to see her little brother living on through his son.

She made the expected rounds to greet the partygoers. Some people she knew, many she didn't. The house looked beautiful. Not much seemed different since the last time she had been there. Wallpaper had been stripped and replaced with paint. Most of the original light fixtures remained intact. Even with some of Tim's renovations, it was like stepping into a time machine and going back to her childhood. She almost expected to see herself and Jimmy hiding under the furniture.

Sarah was deep in a conversation with a distant relative, so Bess wandered off to hit up the hors d'oeuvres table. She picked out a few crackers and a slice of salami then turned to look about the room. Even after all the years that had passed, she felt like she'd just been here.

Stepping into the next room, she had the sudden urge to use the bathroom. Looking for Tim, she could see he was engrossed in conversation across the kitchen, so she found his wife Bethany and asked her where the restroom was.

"Oh, I'm so sorry. Tim hasn't been able to get the toilet working down here yet. I hate to ask, but could you possibly use the one on the second floor."

Bess stalled, but knowing she couldn't hold it any longer, she agreed.

"Oh good, it's the second room on the right. We haven't quite begun work up there yet, so everything is original. Probably why the toilet still functions. They don't make things like they used to, do they?"

"No, they sure don't. Thanks so much, Beth. I'll find it okay."

Bethany, obviously a few stuff drinks in, shot her a bright smile and turned back to her conversation.

"Oh! Bess, one more thing," she pulled open a utility draw and pulled out a flashlight. "Take this just in case. The wiring is old and sometimes the lights can be finicky."

Bess thanked her then made her way back through the crowd of partygoers, still enjoying their drinks and chatting up a storm. She felt out of place with all these younger people, but they were welcoming enough. Passing through the sitting room, she found *the* stairwell, the one she'd last seen as a child while trying to catch up to her mother and brother. It all looked eerily the same.

Beginning her ascent, the treads under her feet let out a familiar creaking sound. It was odd, but that sound made her long to see her mother and brother again. She felt the air get colder as she approached the second story landing.

The dust on the railing was a strange contrast to the rest of her living memory. Reaching for the knob, she paused, then decided against going in.

Second room on the right, she reminded herself.

Thump-Thump-Thump.

Bess stopped moving. Her heart fluttered at the sound of footsteps coming from the ceiling above her.

"It can't be. That's impossible," she said aloud to herself.

THUMP THUMP.

Two louder thumps on the ceiling, as if confirming that her assumptions were correct. Her heart beat rapidly in her chest and she fought the urge to run back downstairs, grab Sarah, and get the hell out of this house—she had to know.

She started towards the stairwell that led up to the attic, passing the bathroom. Suddenly, she'd forgotten all about her need to use the toilet. As she climbed the narrow flight of stairs, the sounds of music began to haunt her from the toy room.

That's just my imagination. My memories coming back to haunt me.

Taking her time, she could see that the door to the attic was shut tight. She might be let off the hook if she couldn't get in.

Finally reaching the small landing, a cold draft blew out from the door that was now ajar, as if welcoming her home.

The door let out a loud squeal as she opened it wider. The darkness felt like a vortex as it tried to pull her in. She clicked on the flashlight and shined it into the abyss. Not much changed up here. It was still as cold as ever, and there were piles of junk stowed away in the corners. Mouse poop and bird feathers littered the floor. *How lovely,* she thought.

She walked toward her destination, the tiny closet-like room and as the beam of light illuminated the door, she was overcome with a heavy sadness.

Now at the door, she waited for the *chugga-chugga* sound of something rapping on the door, though it never came. She waited for the sound of moaning, but it never came. Finally collected, she unlocked the door and lifted the latch that held it shut. This time, there was no putrid smelling feces, urine, or body odor. Just the same dank smell that filled the rest of the attic.

Opening the door, she shined in the light and saw the floral-patterned wallpaper remained intact but had begun to peel and deteriorate in many spots. The painting of the eerie-looking gnome sat on the floor and leaned up against the outer wall where it once hung. The panes of glass still remained in the window overlooking Pleasant Street. *Huh,* Pleasant *Street. How ironic...*

Now a grown woman, the room appeared to be considerably smaller than it had when she was a young girl. This made the idea of a child being locked up in there so much worse. A sense of mourning overwhelmed her and she couldn't shake that old feeling of guilt she dealt with her entire life since that fateful night in 1950.

Bess was thankful to find he was no longer here, in his prison. Of course she knew he wouldn't be, she wasn't even sure he survived the night all those years ago, let alone lived long enough to be a grown man.

Bess pointed the light at the corner where she and Jimmy had first laid eyes on the boy, as he crouched down beside his bucket. What she saw there hurt her almost as much: the bucket— *his* bucket—laid tipped over on the floor. A pair of skinny, plastic legs peeked out from inside. She stepped inside the room and grabbed the doll by the leg for a closer look. Barely able to see through her tears, she stood there in that tiny room brushing the doll's matted hair with her hand.

"I'm sorry. I'm *so* sorry. We should have brought you with us," she said to the doll, as if she'd been speaking to the boy she abandoned.

"I hope you can forg—"

BOOM.

CLICK.

The door behind her slammed shut. Panicked, she gasped as she turned and attempted to push open the door, but it wouldn't budge. She looked around the room with the flashlight and it suddenly felt like the walls were closing in on her.

The window! She could just break the window and hopefully climb out into the attic. She could survive a few cuts and scrapes, but there's no way she'd survive a night stuck here in the cold.

She stepped back and raised the heavy flashlight to smash the glass when a figure stepped out from the shadows and stared at her through the window. Startled, she fell back against the wall, having recognized who it was immediately, *the boy*. Except that was impossible. He looked as though he hadn't aged a day. She shined the light in his direction and saw him for what he really was. His skin was grey and purplish in spots. His teeth were cracked, twisted in a broken smile as he glared at her. His skull on top was caved in as if he'd been bludgeoned to death and one of his eyeballs dangled loosely from its empty socket.

Bess cried in horror, dropping the flashlight as she retreated to the corner. *His* corner. Upon impact, the flashlight turned off, leaving them alone in the darkness. Together once more.

She felt around hoping to find it, but all she could reach was the doll. *His* doll. Afraid to leave her arm extended anymore, she pulled the doll back into her lap and settled into a seated fetal position, ignoring the burning pain in her tired knees.

She could feel his eyes watching her and she didn't like it. She could not move save for her hand that gently stroked the doll's hair. Through the floor she could faintly hear the voice of Bing Crosby crooning to an audience of dolls, blocks, teddy bears, Lincoln Logs, and the rocking horse inside the room full of toys below.

"Bing…"

§

Downstairs, Sarah began to worry as the first floor's attendees were thinning out. She hadn't seen her mother in over an hour, and when Bethany checked the second floor bathroom, she said it looked like it hadn't been used in years. Officially worried, Sarah and Bethany tracked down Tim to help.

The three of them spent the rest of the evening searching the house. Sarah even drove to her mother's house to see if perhaps she'd gotten a ride home without letting anyone know, but she wasn't home. Sarah decided to stay the night at Tim's in case her mother somehow showed up.

§

The next morning, Tim finally came across the body of Bess inside the small room in the attic. She was crouched down in the corner holding a doll. Her lips were purple, and her eyes were frozen shut. Sarah couldn't fathom what drove her mother to go up into the attic in the first place. She recalled her mother's apprehension to go to the house in the first place, like she had a premonition. Sarah's guilt was palpable. Her mother's death left her devastated.

The coroner later reported that she had died from hypothermia.

No one could figure out how she managed to get herself locked in there from inside the room, or why there was a tiny room in the attic to begin with. In the report it remained a mystery, and they chalked it up to being 'an unfortunate accident.'

Tim decided to sell the house to a family before the renovations were complete. It was too painful to go in there knowing what had happened to his aunt.

The family that bought it immediately fell in love with the place after their first walkthrough. Their kids begged them to buy it after they'd discovered the huge room full of vintage toys, so they did just that.

On moving day, the children ran up the stairs to the second floor to inspect what goodies were left behind. Johnny ran up to the collapsed pile of Lincoln Logs and began working on building a castle. The oldest daughter eyed a sturdy rocking horse with excitement until she spotted an old record player in the corner. She walked up to it to see if it still worked.

"Hey Johnny, who's Bing Crosby?"

POLYBUS

Many in the paltry coastal town of Polybus referred to Danforth as the *Puzzle Aficionado*. The clever play on words considerate of his daytime trade as a deep-sea fisherman. While hooks, nets, and bottomless buckets of fish guts stole much of his time beneath the hot sun, tiny peculiarly shaped pieces of painted wood obsessively consumed his sleepless hours under the glow of the moon and the dark infinite of space. When he wasn't fishing for his livelihood, he was puzzling to feed his addiction.

Absent amidst the bustling heat of Summer, the overcast winds of Autumn were accompanied by an influx of free time bestowed by the southern migration of highly sought-after schools of fish that preferred the warmer waters of the southern hemisphere. For most of the residents of Polybus, this was the season of habitual mating, of educating the adolescents, or the fabricating of next season's tackle and netting. Everyone had their purpose, staying busy during the cold nights leading up to the harsh New England winter that often found them storm stayed, but not Danforth.

Having no wife or child to care for, Danforth found the frigid seasons to be his most productive for his admittedly enslaving hobby. Living on the outskirts of the village in a modest, single-room home, no debts were in his name. Surviving off the fish he caught then preserved, wearing secondhand clothing, and burning firewood he hastily gathered for warmth. He spent nearly every cent of his earnings on new and exciting puzzles. The more elaborate and challenging, the better.

Every few weeks, Danforth would hitch a ride to the bustling city of Umbra in search of new puzzles. Stockpiling them in hopes of not having to repeat any. Jigsaw puzzles, considered an insufficient commodity to folks of the time, were inexpensive. To his benefit, Danforth could often return home with several dozen puzzles, satisfying his voracious compulsions while not breaking the bank.

Constantly searching for the one, *the puzzle of puzzles*, he often found himself disappointed by the lack of unique conceptual design and difficulty. No matter where he bartered, the puzzles were all the same. Far-reaching landscapes, cozy homesteads, lush gardens, fantastical worlds existing only in the imagination, or biblical imagery. Neither poverty, nor loneliness, nor death or illness, were among his biggest fears. Boredom of his beloved and most precious pastime was what he feared the most.

§

One October night, long past the usual postal service delivery hours— the only visitor he ever received—a hard rapping sounded on the door. This was peculiar seeing as the mail carrier was never prone to knocking while delivering, nor did he work after sundown.

Danforth, focused on the incomplete replica of the Andes Mountains, looked up from his tabletop with a curious expression. This was an unexpected turn of events and the interruption severed him from his concentration.

His hand hovered over the table pinching a puzzle piece between his thumb and forefinger, before finally finding its home just below the snow cap summit. Hesitant at first, he let out a grunt of annoyance, pushed his chair away from the table, and approached the front door.

He noticed the fire had burned down to nothing but flickering embers, and he grumbled at the sight of the nearly empty firewood rack. He would need to collect a few more logs from the lean-to outside—cutting at least several minutes off his allotted puzzling time.

Having lost his train of thought he stood confused in the center of the room. Another hard tap on the door reminded him right away of why he'd left the table.

"Alright, alright. I'm coming. Hold yer horses!" he called with more than a hint of annoyance in his tone.

Sliding back the burlap curtain, he gazed out the window suspiciously unable to see far beyond the pane of glass.

"Who's there?" No response. "Well, what do ya want?"

Unable to see anyone, he reached back to the table and retrieved the three-tiered candelabrum. He raised the light up to the glass and tried again to see who would dare knock on his door at such an inappropriate hour. Just beyond the glow of the flickering flames, a tall dark figure stood in the shadows, seemingly waiting to be welcomed in by its host. It did not move, the figure seemed to be composed of the very same blackness that enveloped it.

Squinting, Danforth called out, "hello," one last time. Rain trickled down the windowpane in pencil thin streams making it difficult to differentiate who the mysterious figure might be. No stranger would come knocking so late, and on a night like this—it had to be someone familiar.

Annoyed, he slid the curtain back across the window and walked to the door. He opened it slowly at first but was hit by a sharp gust of wind that pulled the door from his grasp, forcing it to slam against the wall. He drew back in surprise as the three candles were snuffed out leaving only the dim glow of the fireplace to insufficiently light the room. Danforth pulled a small box from his pocket, plucked out a match and struck it on the brass doorknob. The wind died down as he relit the wicks, which soon illuminated the entryway sending dancing shadows on the walls and floor.

A thick fog rolled in and formed a barrier between the outdoors and indoors. Not one molecule made its way into the house, the fog clung to the outside as if trapped behind glass. Danforth glared at the odd sight before him, not sure whether to approach it or to slam the door shut. He wasn't fond of unexplainable curiosities, and this was something he'd never witnessed before.

"H-h-hello?" he called, his voice teetering on the edge of nervousness and irritation. "Is anyone th-there?"

The fog curled a few feet away from him as if it was gliding on a sheet of ice. He stepped forward and the candlelight barely penetrated the swirling slate-colored mist. He stood just beyond the doorway for what felt like minutes then he took his hand and swiped at the sea fret. To his surprise, it was plain old nothing-out-of-the-ordinary fog. This confused him even more, but he continued to wave his hand, attempting to clear a path as he stepped out through the doorway.

"Who's out here? I saw you through the window. Please, step into the light, I'm not fond of surprises. Even less so of pranksters," his voice was sharp and not at all warm. He wanted this to be over quickly and knew he wouldn't feel safe with some intruder lingering around the grounds outside his home at night.

He walked forward little by little. "I'm warning you. I'm carrying a firearm and I'm not afraid—" he stopped. The end of his foot found something solid that sat on his doorstep nearly tripping him. He regained his composure then looked in the direction where the figure had been standing. Nothing but darkness amidst the fog.

He bent down with the candelabrum stretched out ahead of him and a wooden box came into focus. It looked ancient and appeared to be waterlogged. Red and green algae encircled a strange emblem and sharp white barnacles jutted out from the edges.

Danforth tilted his head to the side like an inquisitive mongrel. He'd never seen anything like this box which appeared out of nowhere. It looked as though it had been sitting at the bottom of the bay for years, possibly even decades.

He knelt for closer observation. The candlelight dispersed the thick fog as he descended as if it was trying to avoid the flames. The air smelled and tasted salty, almost acidic like vinegar, as if he were out on the water with a hull full of catch that'd gone bad. Reminded of the time he came across a carcass of a humpback which had floated onto the beach. Its side was ripped open by some enormous sea creature and filled with feasting gulls, crabs, and insects. He'd never forgotten the putrid smell that clung to his clothing for days on end after the macabre discovery.

The peculiar emblem engraved into the center of the lid was unfamiliar to him. As he ran his fingertips across the carving, a wet guttural growl echoed from somewhere in the fog. It was a noise he'd never heard in all his days, and it sent goosebumps prickling across his flesh. He waited and listened. His wide eyes darted around in all directions fearing that a vile creature of some unknown origin would jump out and rip him open like the whale. It sounded again, only this time it seemed much closer. Without hesitation, he instinctively reached down and scooped up the box. It was heavier than he'd expected for its size. Inside, he could feel hundreds if not thousands of tiny objects shifting around.

Slowly walking backwards, careful not to lose his footing, he clutched the box to his chest as if it was a precious artifact that required his protection. The flickering candlelight traced his steps back inside while the fog eagerly took its place on the front step.

He pushed the door with his foot slamming it shut and slid the lock into place. The rapid beating of his heart reverberated inside his head like a tribal drum. Danforth's chest was tight, the fear and anticipation that swirled through his veins had only increased since finding this enigma. This ancient-looking receptacle had to have come from somewhere, but *that* was the grand mystery. *From where?*

He returned to the table where he'd spent most of his evening and carefully sat the box down directly on top of the puzzle he'd been working on all day. The partially completed painting of the Andes Mountains suddenly carried much less importance.

Despite the algae and barnacles growing on its surface, it was in immaculate condition. Danforth stared awestruck at the intricate details of the carving though he couldn't quite make out what it was. Some obscene combination of a spider and an octopus with one glaring eye directly in the center of its body. The eye—*that eye*—seemed to be locked onto him, staring into the very depths of his soul with an insatiable hunger. A hunger for death.

His jaw agape, he could feel the box pulling him in.

What mysteries are hidden inside? From what watery treasure trove did you come? How did you find this place? Why me?

As a million thoughts ran circles in his mind, one question never came to pass; *did it mean to do him harm?*

Before he sat down to investigate further, a cold chill in the air reminded him that the fireplace needed tending to. A couple of dry logs remained in the rack which meant he'd have no choice but to go back outside. Believing that horrifying atrocities waited for him on the other side of the door, that seemed like an impossibility lest he be prepared to meet his maker.

The fire would have to wait. He could not resist the hypnotic draw of the box. He needed to know what was inside. He pulled his chair up to the table and sat down. Danforth's gaze never left the carving of that grotesque abomination. He moved the candelabrum closer, there were many more details than he first picked up on.

The spider-like creature appeared to be sitting on a pile of bones. Below the heap was a row of people, bowing in prayer or worship as if it were a kind of deity. The thought caused him to shiver. Above the enormous thing was a rippled line meant to represent water for there was a ship on it.

Danforth was fascinated and at the same time more terrified than he'd ever been in his whole life. *What could this mean?*

He'd had enough—it was time to open the box and solve the mystery for himself. Rubbing his hands together, he reached down and cupped the side of the box. A marvelous sensation like static electricity surged through his fingertips, into his hands, and faded in his forearms before reaching his elbows. He felt powerful.

His hands maneuvered around the sides of the box, feeling for a seam or hinge, but the overgrowth of algae made it difficult. Finally, he moved his hand to the carving. Part of him did not want to get anywhere near the picture on the lid but another part knew he'd find his answer there.

His finger hovered just above the carving for a second before something forced him to press down hard on the eye—*that eye*—which depressed inward and made a metallic *click* as if he had unlocked a door. The sound was too heavy to belong to this box, it sounded as though he opened the heavy door of some long-forgotten tomb. A seam became visible about a quarter of the way down the box. *Aha!* As he slowly lifted the lid with his thumbs, it released a hiss of steam that shared the same pungent odor as the air outside.

To his utmost surprise, what he found inside the box made his heart leap with joy and bang against his chest. It was as if he'd first laid eyes on his soul mate from across the room, only this wasn't a person. It was a puzzle. A puzzle whose pieces were cut into the most peculiar shapes he had ever seen in all his years of puzzling. There had to be close to one thousand pieces. He couldn't quite make out what the picture was supposed to be, but that was what excited him the most. It had finally found him. The puzzle of puzzles.

Suddenly the who, what, where, why, and how of the box's origins were no longer important. He had work to do, and the night was young.

He lifted the surprisingly heavy box with one hand and with the other pushed the nearly complete puzzle he'd been tirelessly working on for days onto the floor like it was dirty laundry.

Like always, he began by searching out the four corner pieces. This was his least favorite part of puzzling because he found it was the easiest part. With a keen eye such as his, this took him no time at all. Nothing about the partial images were decipherable and without dimensions, he had no idea how wide or tall the puzzle would be, so he made an educated guess and moved onto the side pieces.

The weather outside was getting worse, but for some odd reason, he found himself dampened by a cold sweat. He'd lit several more candles around the room since the fire had all but completely gone out. The chill blowing in from the flue made the joints of his hands stiffen and he wished he'd taken a moment earlier in the evening to refill his stack of wood. It was too late now, and something deep inside urged him to go on.

The sides were coming along nicely, and he could just make out some sort of landscape. Part of him became disenchanted as he'd grown tired of boring old landscapes. This couldn't be all the puzzle was sent to him for... So he could put together *another* secluded cabin in the woods, or a castle set off in the distance behind a field of golden wheat and flowers; perhaps a fishing vessel lost at sea. No, there was more to it. He had to keep going.

After less than an hour of hunting for side pieces, the border was complete. Danforth could finally see the bottom had a patch of land, while the middle section was a vast ocean, followed by an overcast sky. It was larger than many of the puzzles he was accustomed to. The width just fit on the inside of his table and the height took up nearly half it. This was quite possibly the largest puzzle he'd ever completed, in size *and* piece count.

Among the pieces he could see what appeared to be sections of a house. Setting them aside, he felt this would be a good place to start. He found it impossibly easy to find the pieces he was looking for. It was as if some supernatural force was guiding him, trying to speed the process along. As if he were chosen. He didn't like the feeling of being helped along, Danforth carried a certain level of pride in his puzzling ability which took years and years to perfect.

He pressed on. The house was coming along and with only a few pieces left to connect, an uneasy feeling began to roll around in his gut. There was something familiar about the house he was piecing together. As he placed the final piece, he was positive he'd known the house; it was his own. The final piece included the crooked shutter that hung outside his picture window. *How?* Danforth stared in disbelief, failing to reassure himself that the image was different, that it wasn't his home, but he knew his assumptions were correct.

Moving on, he sought out the pieces for an odd creature of sorts that he couldn't quite make sense of. Again, the pieces came to him quickly. Their positioning, which at first seemed nonsensical, fit together perfectly. The creature that was forming with the connection of each piece made no sense. This was obviously a fantastical picture, not one rooted in reality. The fact that the artist replicated a sort of primitive form of art helped him come to terms that this was in fact the work of an overactive imagination.

His curiosity peaked, but the cold numbness in his hands was worse. If he continues, he will most certainly need to go outside to retrieve more firewood. At this point, he'd be lucky if he were able to get another fire started, but he had to try.

The image developing before him was too intriguing. He just needed to finish one corner which would fill out the top left quarter of the puzzle and he could go collect logs to burn.

It appeared as though the house was in the center of the puzzle and some mythological monstrosity occupied each corner. He could not comprehend what it all meant or why the puzzle was left at his doorstep, but he had a nagging desire to see it through.

Piece after piece the creature began to take shape. At first, he thought it resembled a whale, but that could not be. This whale had legs. Long, crab-like legs that stuck out from its torso just before its tailfin . An abomination unlike any creature he'd ever seen in all his years as a deep-sea fisherman.

He pressed in the final piece to fill in the whale-like creature just as thunder roared off in the distance stealing his attention. Leaning back to get a good look, the creature was almost comical in its absurdity. A set of enormous pincers that looked as though they could crush an entire fishing fleet were attached to thick, scaly arms. Unexpectedly, the longer he stared at the creature, the more unnerving it became. The sheer size of the thing far off in the distance compared to the house in the foreground seemed disproportionate. It had to be an artistic decision to make it that large, no creature in the sea was that enormous, not even the blue whale. Nor did they have the features of a crustacean.

An unforgiving draft blew down the chimney and out of the fireplace, nearly extinguishing Danforth's candles. The fire couldn't wait any longer. He stood, retrieved his rain jacket from the hook on the wall and left through the front door. The cold crept over him like a blanket while heavy winds settled, and rain steadily fell all around. Off in the horizon, flashes of lightning that were accompanied by crashes of thunder. The storm wasn't moving out; it was heading directly at him.

Rounding the corner to the lean-to, he collected a heavy armful of damp logs to bring inside. He would have a difficult time getting these lit, but he hoped the kindling would take and dry them out enough to catch.

With arms filled with wood, he headed back inside. Another flash of lightning far off in the distance over the bay lit up the sky. A shiver swept down his spine as he spotted the silhouette of some massive thing standing up over the crashing waves. He paused, refusing to believe his eyes. Hoping for another glimpse to prove himself right, that nothing was there. Just a trick of the light. Perhaps a cargo ship some ways off.

Another bright streak of lightning lit the horizon giving the illusion of daytime and he gasped at the colossus still visible in the distance. It appeared to be an enormous, breached whale, hovering high above the water. But no, that wasn't right. He could see long legs as wide as tree-trunks jutting outward at an impossible angle before descending into the black sea. Towards the front end of the creature, a set of thick arms housing massive pincers swiped at the night sky in search of something to destroy. A blowhole sat atop the beast and let out a fierce blast of air and mist. The expulsion sounded eerily similar to the rumble of thunder brought on by the storm. Perhaps that was what he'd been hearing. *Could this creature be responsible for this abnormally harsh weather?* Of course not. Such thoughts were completely irrational.

The cold rain trickled down his cheeks and neck then under the collar of his shirt. Frozen in awe of the behemoth his eyes were glued to, he knew he was apt to catch a deadly cold if he didn't retreat back indoors. He had a hard time breaking the spell he was under, every flash of lightning offered a brief glimpse of one of the most bizarre, magnificent, and equally terrifying things he'd ever laid eyes on.

To the best of his knowledge, no such creature existed in the natural world. It looked to be something a child or artist would conjure up from deep within their imagination, yet here it was, standing tall in the bay a few miles from his home. He could not deny what he was seeing, for this would require him to deny his own eyes and therefore his own sanity.

Another bright flash of lightning lit the horizon and he noticed that the behemoth had shifted positions. No longer could he see its head and tail spanning from east to west—only arms, legs, a narrow torso and the tail fin as it rose up and down. Its large, cavern-like mouth hung agape, making it clear that the whale had turned and was headed toward the shore. Towards his home. Danforth shivered.

With the damp firewood in his arms, he turned away and kicked open the front door. He had his work cut out for him in terms of starting a fire, but the insufferable cold was creeping inside, and he still had much work to do.

The logs were reasonably dry beneath the bark, the kindling caught and was hot enough to burn out the moisture that once saturated the bark. Within minutes, he had built a fire and warmed his bones.

He sat back down at the table to continue his work. That's precisely the moment when he put two and two together. *The whale!* It was the same one he pieced together on the top left corner of his puzzle.

"That's not possible!" he said aloud, squinting his eyes and leaning in closely for a better look. Sure enough, it was an exact replica of what was lying flat on his table. "This is preposterous. I'm just overtired. My mind is playing tricks on me." Another crash of uproarious thunder shook the bones of his humble home, and with that, he was back at it.

The top right corner seemed as good a place as any to jump into. Being a man of what he considered a reasonable amount of intelligence, he assumed the pieces would materialize more otherworldly creatures from the image. Although this concept made him uneasy and a bit nervous, he was too enamored at the idea of something interesting or unique transpiring during his benign existence. The repetitive nature of deep-sea fishing was enough to make any man go insane and the solitary homelife he had intentionally found himself accustomed to wasn't helping either.

The pieces were falling into place rather fluidly. It felt as though the puzzle wanted to be completed and subconsciously directed his hand. More and more, the image came to fruition, and he was almost able to pinpoint what it was before stopping himself.

Standing up, he walked to the wood pile and tossed a few logs onto the bright hot embers. The bitter cold hours of dawn were drawing close, and he could not let it go out again. Stabbing at the coals with his poker, an odd sort of rumbling could be heard off in the distance.

Horses? he thought. *Not at this hour, nor in this weather.*

His mind settled back to his work, he returned to his chair and sought out the last few pieces to finish off the top-right corner. The warmth of the fire made easy work of his task. After setting the final piece in place, he sat back and studied the puzzle. The rumbling in the distance finally made perfect sense; it *was* horses. The puzzle showed a horse drawn carriage ascending from an opening in the dark waters. The horses were as white as the driven snow, each with a mane and tail of deep crimson. Their eyes were empty sockets except the speckle of white—light reflection. In his mind, he envisioned how impressive the horses would look rising out of the sea as they pulled the carriage of pure onyx. The spokes on the wheels were crafted from bones: femurs, forearms and other intricately connected appendages.

What could be inside that carriage? he asked, knowing he did not want the answer.

The hammering hooves got louder. Drowning out the approaching thunder, he heard the whinny of a bucking equine. It could be his lack of sleep or his mind simply playing tricks, but the sound resembled the scream of a woman in peril.

The pounding drew ever closer, and he could feel the floor beneath his feet begin to shake. Danforth grabbed the candelabrum, walked to the window hoping for a glimpse of the passing carriage. More so, he wanted to make sure it kept on its way and didn't stop outside his door.

Nothing was in sight beyond the dribbles of rain that streamed down the exterior of the windowpane like candle wax. His heart beat fervently as he stared out through the glass.

A bright flash of lightning lit up the sky and he could see that whale-like monstrosity was closer to his vicinity. *What does it want?* he thought, finding himself nearer to the undeniable truth that this was either happening, or he'd fallen asleep and found himself inside of a surreal dream.

The sound of horse hooves had ceased. Pressing his face hard against the cold glass, Danforth strained to examine the empty road. He wanted nothing more than to sit back down and continue his work on the puzzle, but his curiosity got the better of him and he rushed to the door. He turned the knob and opened it, greeted once again by the thick fog that had dissipated only an hour ago. He leaned out with the candelabrum in front, still unable to see any more than a few feet ahead.

"H-h-hello?" his trembling voice broke the silence of the night. Seemingly, at his beckoning, the fog mysteriously cleared away. Pulled back into the sea before his eyes. Curling wisps of retreating mist slowly unveiled a carriage black as coal. A team of horses hitched by heavy-looking, rusted chains chomped on bits made of bone. Their white coats encrusted with bits of carmine-colored liquid that looked brown compared to the crimson strands of their manes and tails.

The puzzle. This was the puzzle's doing. Unable to wrap his mind around that truth, he stood in awe of the horrific beauty of the carriage in front of his house. He raised the light to the front of the carriage to see who (if anyone) was driving. Sure enough, a bulking figure sat in the front seat, cloaked in a thick velvety robe of burgundy. The driver sat motionless as if indifferent to having reached their destination. Moments passed before they skillfully reeled back on the reins to settle the team of horses. In doing so, the sleeve of his robe slid below the wrist and revealed a scaley, green hand.

Just then, one of the horses let out an awful shrill whinny that pierced Danforth's ears, almost causing him to drop the candelabrum. He reared back towards the entrance of his home and as he did, a curtain was drawn inside the carriage. Taking a few more steps back, the warmth of the fire against his back was more than welcomed. The door began to open. Whomever the passenger was, they were taking the utmost care not to scare away the man who watched from inside his small house.

Danforth lost his nerve and before he could see who had stepped out onto the street, he slammed the front door and bolted it. He was surprised to discover he was short of breath and had wet himself at some point between opening and closing the door. The warmth soaked inside his pants reaching down to his ankles as he stood there trying to regain his composure. Part of him was afraid to move, as if standing still was holding back the progression of time, and whatever monster was climbing out of that carriage was locked in place. Nothing else made sense, so why shouldn't it be true? His attempt to convince himself was unsuccessful.

Feeling uncomfortable, he moved across the room to his chest of clothing to retrieve a fresh pair of pants, hoping he wouldn't hear a knock on the door. After he was dressed, he swiftly moved to the window and closed the burlap curtain before returning to his work.

Seated back at the table, he glanced down at the hellish carriage and the behemoth amalgamation that hulked over the bay. A wave of fear and uncertainty washed over him for what might be next.

For the briefest of moments, he considered dismantling the puzzle and placing it back inside the cursed wooden box from which it originated then tossing it into the blaze. A voice inside spoke out against this, knowing he could never will himself to destroy such a precious oddity. Or was it a curse in disguise? Someone, or something, dropped this off at his doorstep for a purpose and he knew he would be the one to fulfill that purpose. Plans were in motion, and he would not get in their way.

Setting aside his distracting personal anguish and fear, he grasped the candelabrum and pulled it in close. Searching for the next set of pieces, he worked on the bottom left corner of the puzzle. With fewer pieces to search through, the picture came fast. Piece-by-piece, he was chipped away at the fabric of reality while pulling open a doorway of unknown possibilities his imagination could never conjure up.

As the final pieces were fit into place, an unsettling high-pitched scream ripped through the darkness. Resembling the screeching call of a bird of prey, combined with that of a hungry newborn, it sent a shiver down his damp skin. This was a sound he'd heard before.

The lower corner of the puzzle showed what appeared to be Blackmoss Forest, which bordered the outskirts of Polybus. The trees there grew so dense, stretching on for an undisclosed number of miles. Few ever dared venture into Blackmoss for fear of getting lost, but there were other rumors that also kept the people of Polybus out.

Danforth had traversed the edges of the forest many times throughout his life, testing his luck. On several occasions he'd swore he could hear an animal wailing deep amongst the trees. Other times, it sounded like the cries of a woman in agony. Now this same noise was outside, also heading in his direction.

In the puzzle, the figure was stepping out of the forest and onto the gravel road. Although its body had features that appeared human, others were not. The legs and arms resembled that of a human—hairless rippling calf muscles, biceps and forearms. Massive hands and bare feet. It wore a sash of thorned ivy around its waist that did little to conceal its tree trunk-like genitalia that hung down between its thighs. The torso was the stuff of nightmares. In place of pectoral and abdominal muscles, a face was growing out of the midsection. The face of an anguished infant as though it was starved or midcry. Atop its shoulders was the feathered head of an eagle, its beak wide open. Protruding from the scapula grew a set of outstretched wings that looked more like a bat than a bird. They were covered by veiny flesh and tufts of hair.

Danforth stared into the infantile eyes on the torso as another screeching cry broke through the howling wind. He flinched, bumping into the table causing the legs to rub against the wooden floor planks, shaking the few remaining loose pieces of the puzzle to the floor.

He gathered himself and the puzzle pieces together. A stiff breeze squeezed through the door jamb causing the curtain to shudder like a flag on a ship at sea. His eyes darted to the curtain, then to the door as a loud knocking rattled the hinges.

Danforth shook his head vigorously repeating, "no, no, no," aloud to himself. He knew he must look like a madman sitting in the candlelight in front of his puzzle speaking to himself, but he did not care. He still had work to do.

As he slid the last few pieces into place, the doorknob rattled aggressively as though someone were trying to break in. Wind howled, scraping at the window pane as the floor shook with each footfall of the enormous approaching behemoth.

With the final piece in place, the last picture was clear. He sat and stared, not knowing what to make of it all. Nonetheless, he was finished.

The candlelight flickered as the chaos surrounding him continued despite his oblivious state. Cold, heavy beads of sweat dripped down his forehead, a symptom of his nervousness.

His lack of sleep was finally catching up to him. His vision was beginning to blur, he felt lightheaded. Moving the candelabrum closer, he saw the final picture. Expecting all the while to see some wretched grotesque monster, he was pleasantly surprised by the image of a door.

BANG. BANG. BANG.

A heavy pounding on the door proved to him that he was not alone and whomever was outside wanted to get in. Following the knocking, the ground shuddered, rattling his humble home. A humming noise could be heard coming from outside and he maneuvered over to the window to see if he could identify its source.

The rain had finally stopped, though the morning sun remained hidden behind the drape of the night sky. *That's impossible*, he thought. To his relief, the horse drawn carriage was gone, but in its place stood a straight line of figures wearing crimson hooded cloaks. Unable to see their faces beneath the darkness, he could pinpoint the low humming was in fact coming from these strangers. They were chanting.

BANG. BANG. BANG.

He peered out trying to see who was knocking at his door but had no luck. He closed the curtains, debating whether to go to bed and ignore the strangers or to open the door to get whatever business they had with him finished.

After another more aggressive knock at the door, he determined these people were not going to leave him alone. He retrieved the candelabrum then walked to the door. The hinges cried out for oil as Danforth was overwhelmed by the rancid odor of rotting fish—not too dissimilar from the chum he worked with during fishing season. This smell wasn't carried by the breeze, it came from the tall, cloaked figure that stood before him. The cloak was dark green with golden threading at the seams. Danforth stood motionless in awe of the sheer size and girth of the person who stood in his dooryard. The rest of the figures stopped their chanting and fell silent.

His eyes wide, he managed only seven words (all of which lacked any confidence), "He-hello? Can I help you with something?"

The figure didn't respond at first, but removed its hood, revealing a large, elongated head. He hadn't noticed at first, but the hands of the figure were webbed with sharp claws. Where ears should have been, a set of deep protruding gills aligned the side of the face. Its wide mouth resembled a sea bass', with eyes and a nose that were more human... except the eyes were dark as the bottom of the sea.

When it finally spoke, its deep voice had a slight reverberation to it. Danforth listened intently like each word coming out of the figure's mouth was the most important he'd ever heard. "We never doubted you would be the one to open the gate. To set them free. We've been watching you."

Danforth was dumbfounded. He had no idea what the strange figure was going on about.

"I'm sorry, but it seems you are mistaken."

"Did you not accept our gift? Did you not unlock the secrets contained inside the box?"

Danforth looked back at the table. He could now see an eerie iridescent light emanating from the puzzle that wasn't there before.

In the distance, a loud whale-like cry bellowed out of the darkness. From another direction, the high-pitched scream from earlier tore into Danforth's ear drums.

"There is no time for meaningless conversation. You have started, as was foretold, and now you must finish."

Danforth did not like the sound of this. The horrible cries in the distance continued and the cloaked figures began chanting once more.

"You have opened the gate, but the ritual is not complete. There is one final piece to the puzzle."

"No, no. You're wrong. I finished the puzzle. See for yourself," Danforth explained frantically, pointing to the glowing puzzle on the table. Being a perfectionist, he didn't like this creature's assumptions. "I *have* finished it."

"That's but one piece of the puzzle. The rest is through the door."

"The door? What door?" he was confused, and rightfully so.

"This door," the creature repeated, stepping aside to reveal a door in the middle of the road. Danforth looked at it curiously, he needed to complete the puzzle, but he had no interest in walking through some magical door that manifested out of thin air. Still, a yearning was growing inside of him. A feeling of needing to know. It felt identical to the urges he got when nearing the end of one of his puzzles. Some would call it an addiction, but it was more like an obsession.

"What's behind the door, if you don't mind me asking."

"All the riches a man like yourself could possibly desire; all your dreams coming to fruition. A boundless eternity overflowing with happiness and prosperity," the creature did its best impression of a smile. "Come now. Time is short. They want to meet you. Want to thank you for freeing them from their prison."

"They? Who are they? What's really going on here? None of this is making sense."

"All your questions will be answered. Your fears will be relinquished. All after merely stepping through this door." As the figure said this, a bluish light began emanating from the edges of the door. The mysticism at work was too great for Danforth to resist. "Please."

Danforth stood there, a broken man. Malnourished, overtired, dehydrated, and on top of it all, his hair and beard had been neglected for weeks making him look well beyond his years.

"Riches you say?"

"Everything you could ever desire."

"Well... then...let's get this over with, shall we?"

He approached the door. The candlelight lit the face of the creature, highlighting its scaly flesh. Danforth noted the complete lack of hair. The figure flashed Danforth another wide smile exposing small knife-like teeth.

Something felt very wrong about this, but Danforth pressed on. The row of cloaked figures to his left, all standing motionless on the road. He looked to the right and saw the same. He considered running away, escaping into town to get help, but he knew his exhaustion wouldn't allow it. Besides, it was quite apparent these people dealt in some form of ancient black magic. He was trapped.

Trembling, his stiff fingers hesitantly closed around the door knob. He noticed the same glaring eye—*that eye*—staring back at him, only this time it was looking back. He turned the knob, looked back at the hulking figure one last time, pushed open the door, and took a step inside.

At first, he saw nothing but blinding blue light. His eyes adjusted and recognized he was in an enormous torchlit chamber made of what appeared to be coral. Massive sketches of monstrous, mythical sea creatures decorated the imperfect walls. In front of him sat an altar, rusted shackles hung down at its side. On one side of the altar was a looming statue of the whale-like monster he'd seemingly released from the puzzle. On the opposite side was a statue of the great winged monster he'd only heard but recalled its likeness as represented on the puzzle. *Gods?* Behind the altar sat a large figure—twice the size of the creature that coaxed him here—sitting on a throne of large bones. In his hand, a long blade gleamed.

Danforth's heart dropped to his stomach, his eyes welled with tears. He quickly turned around to exit through the door from which he'd entered but was met with the large fish-like creature. The door vanished. There was no escape. Danforth whimpered as salty tears ran down his cheeks. He mourned, though not for fear of losing *his* life, but understanding that he would never complete another puzzle.

The booming voice of the seated figure echoed off the walls of the chamber, sending a chill down Danforth's spine.

"Join us at the altar, *you* are the final piece."

The figures around the room cheered and clapped in celebration, overpowering Danforth's desperate cries for help as he was dragged to the altar to finally complete the ancient puzzle.

THE BLUE CLIFFS

Gabriel could smell the sea as he parked his car. To his delight, the lot was empty save for one car that looked to be an antique. Most beachgoers were still at home asleep with their families at this hour. That would make this much easier.

He looked around the inside of his '02 Honda Civic. The passenger seat was covered with grey and white hair. A thin strip of dirt gathered at the crease in the bottom of the cushion. Translucent nose prints were speckled across the windshield and passenger side window. He traced his fingers along the seat and pinched a couple tufts of hair then raised it to his face.

"I love you, girl. You'll be fine. They'll find you a good home."

He let the hair fall back onto the seat and a small two-by-four inch picture of a young boy nestled into the corner of his rearview mirror stole his attention. Pulling gently, he separated the photograph from the small curl of scotch tape that held it in place on the mirror. *Benny.* A name that carried with it pain and anguish, now sounded almost heartening, knowing he might get a chance to see his little brother again. Perhaps sooner than later.

Reaching up to replace the photograph, he changed his mind and slid it carefully into the breast pocket of his shirt. Eyes closed, he patted the pocket as if to say *you'll be safe in there, Benny.*

Glancing one more time around the vehicle's interior, he took in the years of memories this old car gifted him. Trips to Boston, driving to school jamming out to pop songs on the radio, changing a flat tire in the pouring rain, Lola's big ears flopping around as she stuck her head out the window, Benny's eyes lighting up as he looked out, watching the beautiful coastal scenery rush by on the way to the beach with his big brother. Gabriel winced at the painful memory, pulled the keys out of the ignition, and swung open the door.

The gravel under his feet sounded intrusive amongst the quiet stillness of dusk. A light breeze was blowing. Stars were still visible, although barely, as they awaited the arrival of the August sunrise.

Goosebumps crawled up Gabriel's arms as he set his keyring down against the windshield wiper. He turned, stopping abruptly as he remembered the letter he'd painstakingly scrawled the evening prior. Although rain wasn't in the forecast, he had slipped the letter into a Ziplock bag in case it took a few days for anyone to find it. He tucked it carefully under the wiper beside his keyring.

Placing his hand on the hood of his car, he felt the warmth of the engine beginning to cool in the chill of the early morning air. He gave it a light tap before taking to the path he'd walked a couple weeks prior.

Gabriel looked up at the diminishing stars, he felt a rush of warm wind blow past his legs. For a moment he thought it might be Benny excitedly running ahead to catch a glimpse of the powerful, white-crested waves crashing against the rocks. Or perhaps to find the elusive sand dollar he'd been wanting so badly before his brother snatched it up. The latter strictly for bragging rights. But that was impossible. He knew it wasn't Benny. It was just the wind playing tricks on him. Taunting him. Maybe even guiding him to where he belonged.

Eyes gazing back up at the infinite skyscape of stars, he caught sight of a shooting star as it made its way across the horizon before disappearing into the vast ocean below. He knew it never found its way into the sea, and that it was far off in the depths of space. Still, his wandering mind imagined what it would be like to be on a ship miles out and see a meteor splash into nearby waters.

Did you see that, Benny? You love shooting stars, don't you?

As he came back down to Earth, his shins met with the thicket of wild roses that bordered the trail. Those tiny thorns couldn't penetrate the denim of his blue jeans, but it startled him, nonetheless. Gathering his bearings, he continued down the path, passing by a wooden bench that overlooked the cliffs up ahead.

His mind wandered back to Benny. Finally catching up to him as he stopped to bounce back and forth along the seat of the bench. It was always a joy to see his little brother make something out of nothing. A prosaic object as benign as a park bench could transform into a playground inside the spectacular mind of a child. *At what point in life did I lose that sense of wonder and imagination? Perhaps it's something intentionally let go for fear of being perceived as immature... such a shame to lose so much of who we were just to be accepted by those who'll never accept us anyway.* Benny never lost that innocence. In a way, he was lucky.

Passing by the bench, Gabriel walked the short distance that brought him to the wooden guardrail lining the steep embankment known as The Blue Cliffs. The name was given thanks to the wall of blue sky above and dark blue ocean below that visitors were met with as they approached the embankment of jagged barnacle-covered rocks below. Locals knew it had another meaning. The *blue* also reflected the depressed state of mind that hundreds of people felt before jumping to their deaths throughout the years. Gabriel was no different.

As he stood on the precipice of his demise, he closed his eyes tightly and thought back to the day of the accident. Benny, who'd grown bored of playing on the bench, was on his knees picking through the bramble of wild roses that peeked out from below the guardrail. Fascinated by the pieces of seashells and smooth stones he found; a bright red feather stole his attention. Gabriel sat on the bench, watching in awe of his brother's inquisitive nature. Off to his left, a family was approaching down the path carrying towels and a cooler. Gabriel smiled and waved. The assumed mother reacted with a look of sheer terror as she dropped her belongings and pointed ahead. Gabriel never heard her scream as he turned just in time to see Benny tumble off the guardrail, falling head first onto the rocks below.

One last visit to the memory that haunted him for all this time would help to seal the deal. No turning back now.

A thought crossed Gabriel's mind as he stood there in the stillness of the morning. *Perhaps he can stick around for one more sunrise. NO!* He couldn't grant himself even one more Earthly delight as he worried it would convince him to change his mind. He didn't deserve it—what he deserved was the fate that beckoned him down below.

The crashing of waves below was soothing as it called his name. He could hardly see the glistening ripples from the moonlight that would soon burn away from the sunshine.

Carefully, he made his way onto the guardrail knees first, then onto his feet. Finding it difficult to balance on the wooden beam, the sound of the coaxing waves pulled at his shoulders, welcoming him into the chilly waters and sharp rocks below.

The blushes of pink and orange stretched across the horizon with oncoming daylight, saying farewell to the dark blue hues of the night. The beauty of the moment brought tears to his eyes before the full appreciation of what he was about to do forced them into a gushing flow of emotion.

The Blue Cliffs were living up to their name. Gabriel sought the courage to bring it all tumbling down to a crashing smattering of broken bones and ultimately death; he took in a few deep breaths. His heart was beating so heavily the breaking waves were muted, and the whispering wind felt like a gentle prickle against his bare skin. It was now or never.

Goodbye, Benny. I'll see you soon, brother. I love y—

"You don't want to do that." A youthful yet somehow lifeless voice broke through his hypnosis, and he nearly lost his balance on the beam.

"What the...?" Gabriel looked around for a moment but saw nobody. Almost missing the young man seated on the bench. His legs were crossed, and he was dressed in untimely attire. His laid-back posture was one of indifference in contrast to the serious situation taking place. "What are you doing there? I mean... where'd you come from?"

"*I've* been here the whole time. What is it that *you* are doing?"

Gabriel's confusion shifted to annoyance, "That's none of your damn business, man. Now how about you move along and leave me alone."

The man pondered this directive while rubbing his smooth chin, "Well... I could do that, except I'm no fool. I wouldn't be able to *live* with myself knowing I willingly let a man end his own life without at least attempting to talk him out of it."

Gabriel did his best to look insulted knowing damn well the stranger was correct in his assumption. "Look, you don't know what you're talking about, *pal*. I've come to say goodbye to my brother."

"Benny? Is that it?"

Gabriel eyed the stranger suspiciously, trying to remember if he'd said his brother's name aloud since he'd arrived.

"How do you know his name? Who are you?"

"Ah yes, Benny. I've seen him around here a few times as of late. Cute kid! Inquisitive nature about him. Reminds me of myself at that age. Many, many years ago."

"Oh come on...You're pulling my leg. You can't be more than eighteen years old."

"Seventeen actually. I was turning eighteen a few weeks after it happened. I had just gotten my driver's license and my parents bought me my first car. A well-loved 1960 Buick station wagon. A hand-me-down, but boy did I love that car!"

"Wait... is that your rig up in the parking lot?"

"Did ya see it?"

"The pukey green antique?"

"Yeah, that's it. Beauty ain't she? I was looking forward to taking Michele to the Snowball this winter. We used to go for rides around the neighborhood and I'd sing her that song, *Michelle, ma Belle,* from the new Beatles album. Couldn't carry a tune with a team of oxen but it made her laugh. She was so beautiful when she laughed."

"You *are* pulling my leg, man. The Beatles haven't had a new album since 1970 just before they broke up."

"Broke up? Now you're the one pulling my leg," he paused. "Oh that's right. Sometimes I forget about what happened. I get so caught up in memories. Life always marches on, now, doesn't it?"

Gabriel hopped down off the guardrail and scratched at his head. He took a seat on the beam of wood with his back to The Blue Cliffs. "So what is this all about, anyways? Is this some kind of joke?"

"No joke, sir. Just don't get many visitors this time of day and ya know, it's nice to be able to have a conversation once in a while. It gets lonely up here sometimes. We all need someone to talk to, even if it's just in passing. Speaking of loneliness, how's your mother doing? It must have been so hard for her to lose her baby boy."

A hot feeling of anger rushed through Gabriel before it was washed away by his lingering sadness. *Who is this guy to be asking about our mother?*

"She's not doing too well. Even after all these weeks, she still hasn't forgiven me for what happened. It's hard to be in the house with her sometimes. I can hear her sitting in Benny's bedroom, talking to him like he's still there. Like he's...still alive. But he's not, and it's my fault! She knows it, and I know it!"

"Ah yes, of course. So you must have pushed him then, is that it? You were tired of having a little brother that followed you around, made you laugh, wanted to be just like you? He climbed onto that guardrail, and you said, 'hell with it,' and gave him a good hard shove. Is that what happened?"

Tears returned to Gabriel's eyes as he relived that horrible scene over again. One moment his brother was searching for rocks and seashells, the ocean breeze blew through his dirty blonde hair. Benny's broken body laid motionless on the stacks below. The harsh waves of the Atlantic crashed onto his small lifeless body, pulling him closer and closer to the dark waters.

"I did not push him! I loved Benny! I still love him more than anything! If I could, I would trade my life for his in a heartbeat!"

"Then why do you blame yourself, Gabriel?"

"Because *I* was responsible for him! *I* brought him to the beach. My mom trusted me with her baby, and *I* let him get too close to the rocks. Don't you get it?"

"No. No, I don't get it. Accidents happen, my friend. Fate has a way of doing what it wants with us. That doesn't mean you get to give up."

The stranger uncrossed his legs and rested his elbows on his knees.

"Do you honestly think that will help your mother's pain and suffering?

When she gets a call from the authorities that her oldest son took his own life on the same Blue Cliffs where her baby lost his? Have you such a poor understanding of how precious life is? What about Lola? What'll happen to her? How long will she survive in her cage at the kennel? Heartbroken and lonely, waiting for Gabriel to come pick her up and bring her home."

These thoughts tore Gabriel's heart in two. He hadn't quite thought of the repercussions his death would have on the ones that loved him. Relied on him. "I don't deserve to live anymore. Benny should be alive. He should be here with me right now."

"Oh but he is, my friend. He is *always* with you. Right here," the stranger said, pointing to his heart.

"Come on, you know what I mean. He should be alive, playing with his friends, climbing trees, riding bikes, watching cartoons, looking for sand dollars, terrorizing his big brother. Instead he's—"

"There's something you need to come to terms with, Gabriel. Life is short and it's precious. Lots of people die young and damn it, it's not fair. But what do you think those people would say to you right now if they saw a healthy young man with his whole life ahead of him trying to cut it short because of a little guilt? What do you think Benny would say?"

"Benny wouldn't want me to jump. It's just... the guilt is so damn hard to live with. Every time I look into my mother's eyes, the pain starts all over again."

"Of course it does, and she's hurting too. But losing her first born certainly won't make that pain go away for either of you. I promise you that."

Gabriel sat quietly and stared down at the wild roses, he swung his legs as they dangled off the guardrail. The darkness was slowly evading but he took little notice of it. He was pondering life and death and what it all meant. Nearby, a bird loudly chirped high up in a tree followed shortly by another.

Gabriel looked up and asked, "How do you know so much about this stuff? You can't be much older than I am. Hell, I don't even know your name."

"My friends call me Sam. Well, my old friends did. Kind of a loner nowadays. Let's just say I have a vested interest in this stuff."

"Well, I don't know what to do, Sam. I'm lost. Everything you said is true, but something deep down inside just won't let me forgive myself. Can I live with that until I'm an old man?"

"I can't answer that for you, Gabriel. All I know is you have a lot to live for, whether you know it right now or not. Things will get better. Your wounds will heal. So will your mother's. Right now you two need each other more than ever."

Gabriel sat and contemplated once more. His mind was made up when he'd first arrived but now—now he was having serious doubts. Benny's smiling face complete with his chipped tooth and cheeks full of freckles flashed in his memory and the pain stuck him like a knife to the chest. He winced and rubbed his brow. Sam noticed, but what he saw otherwise gave him an idea.

"Gabriel, I have to get going real soon. It's truly been the honor of a lifetime having this conversation with you under these fading stars. Before you make any final decisions, could you just do me one favor?"

Gabriel looked at Sam, fingers pacing briskly around his chin. Was this guy really asking him for a favor? Was this some sort of distraction?

"Sure Sam, I guess. What is it?"

"Stand up and turn around," Sam said, a gentle smile etched across his face.

"That's it?"

"That's it. Then I'll be on my way, and you are free to do as you choose."

Gabriel furrowed his brow, planted his feet in the dirt, gave Sam a skeptical side glance, then turned around.

What he saw was the sunrise. It stole his breath and his eyes widened at the sight before him. A great white ball rose over the horizon amidst a spray of golden rays that reached up into the pale blue sky and snow-white clouds that sat motionless as if they'd been painted there. The ocean stretched on to eternity with foam-crested waves breaking every so often before crashing into the sea stacks off the Blue Cliffs, sending a rush of salt water into the breeze.

Gabriel was unable to take his eyes off of it. He'd never seen such a magnificent thing in all his life. He was awestruck and for the first time in a long time, was overcome with a calming sense of peace. Warmth rose up the side of his body and to his surprise, wrapped itself around his right hand. It was Benny. He had no doubt in his mind that his brother was there beside him, holding his hand one last time to tell him it was okay. That *he* was okay.

A gleam of sunrise reflected in his eyes as they flooded with tears. They were tears of release. Tears of moving on. He knew he would have to one day forgive himself for what happened and feeling Benny beside him at that moment, he knew the time was now. He thought of his mother sitting at home wrapped in a blanket in the recliner, having fallen asleep watching television. He thought of Lola pacing around the house, looking out the window, worrying and wondering why Daddy wasn't home. He thought of his friends and how they'd tried so hard to comfort him after the accident and how he'd pushed them away. Then his thoughts turned to Sam; the stranger who just might have saved his life.

"I love you, Benny. I'm so sorry for what happened to you. I'll never forget you, please don't forget me. You'll always be my little brother," the warmth in his hand tightened before gently being carried off with the sea breeze and into the sunrise.

He sat for a moment longer before turning back to address his savior. "I've made a final decision. I'm going to—" but no one was there. The bench was empty, and the only sounds were the crashing of the waves below and the chorus of birds waking up in their nests. "Sam? Hey Sam, where'd ya go?" He looked up and down the path but there was no one in sight. No footprints. *Nothing.*

Gabriel said goodbye to his little brother one last time. He felt stronger and, in a sense, wiser. He knew what he had to do.

He started back down the path from which he'd come, and he glanced down at the bench. There was an engraving on the back he'd never noticed before.

§

In Loving Memory of Samuel Thompson
1947-1965

§

My friends call me Sam.
Placing his hand on the bench, he said a final goodbye to the stranger. "Goodbye, my friend. Thank you for saving me."

He left the memorial and noticed a stranger standing beside his Honda Civic. He thought it might be Sam, but quickly realized it was a woman with a tripod at her feet and a camera bag hanging from her shoulder. In her hand was a Ziplock bag and a keyring. She was reading his letter.

His footsteps caught her attention and she turned, clearly spooked by the approaching man.

"Good morning, Ma'am." Gabriel said, greeting her with a warm smile.

"Good morning to you, young man. Is this—" she held up the letter.

"Ah yes, you found my keys! Thank you so much. I've been out here all morning looking for them."

She eyed him curiously, handing him the keys and the letter.

"I hate to be rude, but if you hurry, you might catch the most gorgeous sunrise I've ever seen," he said, eyes shifting down to her camera bag.

Still looking confused, she thanked him and returned his smile. She handed him the letter and the baggy then headed down the side path that went directly to the sandy beach, away from The Blue Cliffs.

Gabriel crumpled up the letter and stuffed it into his pocket. He twirled the keyring on his finger and with his free hand, gently tapped the hood of his car.

"Wha'dya say we get out of here, huh girl?"

As he reached for the door handle, he noticed that the antique puke-green Buick station wagon was no longer in the parking lot. *Sam.* He smiled and opened the door. Once inside, he pulled out the photograph of Benny from his breast pocket and stuck it back to his rearview mirror where it belonged. He looked down at the hair in his passenger seat. "I'm coming home, girl."

He started the car, shifted it into reverse, and looked into the rearview to back out. His heart jumped at the sight in the mirror. Benny was sitting there, staring excitedly out the window before turning his gaze to the mirror. Gabriel saw Benny looking back at him. He smiled at him with his chipped tooth and freckled cheeks, waved a hand, then vanished.

Gabriel quietly pulled out of his parking spot and left The Blue Cliffs, leaving behind Benny and Sam, but never forgetting either of them for the rest of his life.

Please ask for help!

IF YOU OR SOMEONE YOU KNOW IS IN CRISIS, PLEASE
CONTACT THE NATIONAL SUICIDE PREVENTION HOTLINE
1-800-273-TALK (8255)

THE CAULDRON

Norman was a horror movie fanatic, so when a seventh grader approached, telling him he wanted to show him something creepy in the woods, it didn't take much convincing.

"A cauldron? Like a *real* cast iron cauldron? No way. Where is it?" Norman asked outside Birchwood Middle School. He couldn't believe it. This was exactly the sort of thing he needed for his Instagram page. The cemetery photos weren't getting much attention as of late and he worried he might start losing followers.

"Sure is! My dad and I were out on a hike this weekend. We accidentally went off the trail and came across it in the woods. It was *so* cool and creepy. Looks like it's been out there a hundred years or more, but there's really no way of telling. I thought of you immediately, being a horror movie buff and all. You have that cool Instagram page, don't ya?" Trevor asked. His long jet-black hair resembled an oil derrick spilling over his deathly pale skin. He looked almost comical standing next to Norman with his strawberry blonde bowl-cut and blue eyes. Like the biblical representation of temptation vs conscience, angelic and devious.

"That's me. Though I'm not really big into witches, they're kind of girly. But, you have my attention. What trail did you say?" Norman tried to play it cool, but deep down he was jumping for joy. He loved photographing spooky places like abandoned houses and cemeteries, but there were only so many to be found in his town. His dream was to produce horror movies after he graduated from high school in six years. An old cauldron in the woods was right up his alley, girly or not.

"It's a bit of a hike heading northeast off the Pineseed Nature Trail, but I bet I could find it again," Trevor said. "Like I mentioned, we found it by accident."

"Can we go this afternoon? I have video production the rest of the week after school but I'm free today." Norman was having a hard time keeping his cool. He was familiar with the Pineseed Trail, but he'd never been out there. As much as he loved scary stuff, trails running off deep into the woods were just a bit too creepy. Too real. The air of mystery was intriguing to him. He didn't know Trevor that well, being a grade below him, but he seemed trustworthy enough. The flaming pentagram emblazoned on Trevor's black t-shirt convinced Norman that they had similar interests.

"Sure, man. My old man works late today anyway. Don't you have to ask your parents or something?"

"Nah. I'm always doing something after school so my parents will think nothing of it. Besides, it shouldn't take that long, right?"

"I mean, it's no walk in the park, but we should be back before dark. Meet me at the trail in 30 minutes," Trevor said.

"Got it. Gives me time to run home and grab my camera," Norman excitedly hopped onto the bus then turned, "awesome shirt by the way!" He flashed Trevor the sign of the devil and stuck out his tongue. Trevor returned the hand gesture, but Norman was oblivious to the hint of mock sarcasm in Trevor's expression. After he was seated, the door shut, and the airbrakes let out a hiss. Trevor watched as Norman waved goodbye through the window as the bus rolled away. Trevor returned a crooked smile. A crisp gust of October wind blew a heap of dead leaves over Trevor's boots. He always loved the fall and the accompanying scents of burning firewood.

§

Twenty-five minutes later, Trevor spotted Norman jogging up the street to meet him at the trail. A digital camera hanging from his neck, swaying with each footfall.

"Sweet camera," Trevor said.

"I came as quickly as I could. Had to let the dog out and grab this," he said, lifting the digital camera. "Didn't want to keep you waiting." He'd all but given up the disinterested act.

"Right on, let's get going before it gets dark."

"Lead the way," Norman said eagerly.

§

They'd been hiking for close to 40 minutes. The sound of dead leaves and twigs crunched beneath their feet. An old birch tree lying across the path was evidence that the trail wasn't a priority for the town to maintain. Norman started to get anxious as he knew the sun would be setting soon and they hadn't even reached the cauldron yet.

"Not much farther. We veered off shortly after the fallen birch chasing a cardinal. My dad loves birdwatching," Trevor explained.

Norman replied with a mock snoring sound, "How boring. I guess it beats watching the home shopping network like my mom does."

"Yea, I guess it does," Trevor agreed, "say, what's your deal with witches anyway?"

"I don't know," Norman thought for a moment, "I guess the idea of some crazy old woman living in the woods isn't that scary to me. We learned about the Salem witch trials in school, but that turned out to be a big hoax. Plus, there's never been a scary witch movie. Like, *ever*."

"This is where we turn off. Probably 10 more minutes and we're there." Trevor decided to press the subject further, "so what, you don't believe in black magic? Alchemy? Curses? *None of that*?"

"Nah. It's all just make believe. I love horror movies because they're scary, but at the end of the day, they're just stories," Norman said matter-of-factly. "Humans are the real monsters. Even Stephen King says so."

With a smirk, Trevor pointed ahead, "We kept heading this way. I remember this grouping of trees. Let's go."

§

They stayed quiet for the remainder of the hike, the excitement building within Norman. The high-pitched *chip-chip* of a northern cardinal could be heard close-by.

"I think it's up here," Trevor said, breaking the silence, "yep, come this way."

Norman grasped his camera and tried peering up over Trevor's shoulders, but he was just a bit too short. They passed the grouping of trees and to Norman's surprise, a dilapidated cabin that looked to be over 100 years old came into view. It was nestled amongst a group of tall oak trees that were topped with a fiery red-orange foliage. Green moss crept up the walls of the cabin and the loosely hung front door was ajar.

"*Whoa!*" Norman sounded ecstatic. "You didn't tell me about this!" He jogged ahead of Trevor to get a closer look.

"It was a surprise. Pretty sweet, huh? D'ya like it?" Trevor asked, pointing again. "The cauldron is in there."

Norman had begun snapping pictures from different angles. The flash of his camera lit up the clearing as the sun set lower. The shadows of the trees increased the creep-factor, making for the perfect setting.

"*DO* I? Let's go in." Norman snapped a few more shots approaching the cabin. His flash illuminated the intricate details of the moss coated rotting wood. These were bound to go viral. With the right hashtags, his Instagram page would blow up overnight.

Keeping his camera at the ready, the soft wood felt damp as he pushed the door open. Its hinges cried out for oil, barely able to hang onto the waterlogged door. Trevor, seemingly pleased with his new friend's reaction, lagged behind.

Norman was enthralled by what he saw inside. In the corner was a rocking chair. One of the arm rests had rotted off and fallen to the floor. He snapped a few shots. Shadows danced about the room with each flash of the camera. A shelf, thick with dust, protruded from the wall. Glass mason jars filled with reddish-amber liquids sat atop the shelf in a row. His flash lit up the room. The cabin had grown so dark he could barely make out what he'd gone in there for. Another flash revealed a large black cauldron in the center of the room.

"*Wow,* there it is. Trevor, it's here. Where'd ya go, man?" Norman called, too enthralled to realize that no response came from the seventh grader.

Kneeling down onto the floor to attempt an artsy low angle shot, his camera flashed. His heart skipped a beat as he thought he spotted someone in his digital viewfinder. *Trevor?* Hesitantly pressing the shutter-release one more time, the cabin lit up with a bright white flash.

Out of nowhere, the door to the cabin closed and he heard the cast-iron latch drop, locking him inside and making it considerably darker.

"Hey Trevor, *ha-ha,* you can let me out now," Norman said, pretending not to be scared. He found his way to the door and pushed on it. The wood creaked under his weight but wouldn't budge. "Come on, Trevor. This isn't funny!" He desperately cried out while pounding on the door with his fist.

"I think there's someone in here with—" Norman's plea for mercy was cut short as a scream of terror escaped his mouth. The camera dropped to the floor.

§

Standing outside in the fast-approaching dusk, the pounding on the door stopped and Trevor heard a choked gasping sound from inside the cabin, followed shortly by silence. He mocked the sound as he pushed open the door. Walking into the dark cabin without a care, his foot found Norman's digital camera first. Trevor picked it up and slung the strap around his own neck. With his thumb, he wiped the fresh blood from the LCD screen and looked at the first image; the last picture that Norman would ever take. It was of a disheveled old woman in a hooded grey cloak. Her broken yellow teeth enwreathed by flakey cracked lips. Her boney hands with long jagged fingernails were outstretched towards the camera. Her incensed expression was the last thing Norman Wallace ever saw.

"Humph...You sounded scared to me," Trevor scoffed. "Love you, Grandma. See you next year." Walking out of the cabin, he thumbed through the photos on Norman's camera.

"These should get a ton of likes on my Instagram. Thanks, Norm," he said, as he carefully shut the door behind him, this time leaving it unlocked.

He started on his way back to town contemplating how he'd go about forging a runaway letter. The delightful scent of burning logs teased his senses. As he passed the grouping of trees, he heard the *chip-chip* of a cardinal nearby, and he knew he'd done a good thing.

MEAN OLD MR. AMESBURY

June 7, 1974

Scott Amesbury was halfway into a twelver as he headed down the trail carrying a cooler full of beer and ice. Being a star athlete who'd just graduated only hours before, he had plenty of cause for celebration. Scott wasn't much of a drinker, so the cans of Bud were making him light on his feet and warm in the belly.

As he approached the end of the trail, he heard Skynyrd blaring through the trees which likely meant his best friend Kip was already at the party. The acoustics of the quarry amplified the music. The granite walls made for a perfect organic stereo. This, and the fact the woods off Beech Street were incredibly isolated, made it *the* spot for high school parties.

Kip's attention was turned away from Amber Berland's bikini as he heard Scott belligerently singing along to *Gimme Three Steps* as he joined his classmates.

"Scott!" Kip yelled, raising his warm bottle of beer into the air. The crowd of teenagers scattered around the woods that bordered the edge of the quarry, acknowledging his presence with celebratory swigs of whatever they were drinking. The heavy smell of booze and marijuana smoke hung in the air.

"Let's get this party started!" Scott called back, setting the cooler down and pulling out a cold brew. He took a deep gulp off the can and walked over to Kip.

"Why aren't y'all swimming yet?"

"We were waiting for you, man," Kip said. He leaned into Scott and cupped his hand around his mouth. "Not that it's been all that bad outside of the water." He motioned his eyes toward Amber and her friends as they sat on a rock taking shots of tequila in bikini tops and jean shorts.

Scott shot him a wide smile and pulled his Burnchester High t-shirt over his head, tossing it onto the ground. He chugged the rest of his beer, dropped the can beside the cooler, and walked over to the group of guys that were passing around a joint.

"Let me get a hit off that, fellas," Scott asked, trying not to slur his speech.

"Scott, you sure about that man?" A kid named Trevor asked. Blowing out a hit, he hesitantly held out the joint. "You don't even smoke, do ya?"

"Come on, Trev. Is this not a party?" Scott asked, mockingly. "We're officially adults now!"

"Alright, dude. Here ya go."

Scott pinched the joint between his fingers, lifted it to his lips, and inhaled deeply. Almost immediately reeling back, he let out a series of gasping coughs that reverberated off the quarry walls. A string of drool fell from his lips.

The group of smokers couldn't help but laugh upon seeing the captain of the swim team coughing up a lung after one hit.

"A one-hit wonder!" one toker in a tie dyed t-shirt joked.

Scott passed the joint back to the next guy in the circle and joined in on the laughter, intermittently coughing out puffs of smoke until he finally caught his breath. He playfully slapped one of the smokers on the shoulder and turned back towards Kip and the girls.

"Now we can really get this party started!" Scott called out.

On the radio, the DJ introduced the next song and Scott awkwardly dance-walked his way back to Kip as *Come and Get Your Love* by Redbone filled the air.

"Who's going swimming with me?" Scott called out.

Kip saw Scott was half in the bag, and Kip's worry was written all over his face. Scott wasn't used to this level of intoxication.

"Scott, my man. Why don't we chill out for a bit? You're not used to—"

"Hell no! We just *graduated* fucking *high school*, man! It's time to celebrate, Kippy. Who's coming with me?" Scott asked, his bloodshot eyes wobbling their way over to Amber and her friends.

"Heck yeah, let's go swimming!" Amber said, setting down the bottle and sliding off the rock. Her friends followed.

"That's the spirit!" said Scott.

Kip sighed but hung back to watch. Scott walked to the part of the trail overlooking the jumping point that led down into clear water. Amber and her bubbly friends lined up behind him and all the partygoers circled around to watch the first group jump into the water. In Burnchester this tradition was seen as the official beginning of summer.

"Listen up! Listen up!" Scott called out. "Let's hear it for the class of 1974! We made it, and the world is our oyster. Now let's go shuck that bitch! To the future!"

"*TO THE FUTURE!*" The rest called back, cheering and toasting with their preferred intoxicant.

"Scott..." Kip said but was ignored.

Scott looked back at his best friend and smiled.

"LET'S GOOO!" Scott yelled, jogging to the quarry's edge. Taking long strides to clear the ledge below, the heel of his foot found a spot of wet mud where someone spilled their drink. Scott lost his balance, sending him tumbling over the edge head over heels.

Kip was the first to look, followed quickly by the rest of the party. Paralyzed with fear at the sight of his best friend in a crumpled heap, he could do nothing but watch on as blood from the fracture in Scott's skull leaked onto the ledge. His lifeless green eyes forever staring off into the bright blue sky.

"*SCOTT!*" Kip cried as the rest of his classmates panicked, running down the trail—sure not to leave the booze or radio behind. The dulcet tones of Redbone faded off into the woods, leaving Kip alone, sobbing thirty feet over his best friend's dead body.

The call of a nearby blue jay fell on deaf ears.

§

Following the accident, Scott's father held a grudge with the youth of Burnchester—he blamed them for what happened to his only son. He owned the property the trail was on, so he installed a jersey barrier at the mouth of the path that led to the quarry. He spray painted 'NO TRESPASSING!' in bold red lettering to hammer home the point.

For the years following, Mr. Amesbury was known to sit on his front porch—drunk as a skunk—in nothing but torn shorts and a loaded shotgun resting across his lap. Of course, he'd never shot anyone, but that didn't mean his threats weren't convincing enough to keep most of the kids away. At least... for a while.

§

July 1998

My friends and I decided to take our chances one scorching day in mid-July as we had many times before. We'd grown accustomed to mean old Mr. Amesbury's empty threats and were no longer scared of him. It became sort of a game to us.

Myself and two best friends, Stan and Kelly, started towards Beech Street in our bathing suits and sneakers with towels slung over our shoulders. Stan carried a boombox with him everywhere we went. The upbeat summer sounds of *Ace of Base* cut through the humidity, clashing with the grim scenery provided by the unkemptness of Beech Street.

"Turn that down, man. Mr. Amesbury's house is right there," I knew I sounded like a wuss, but I just wanted to go swimming at the Basin without any trouble.

"I'm not scared of that old goat. He can pound sand for all I care," Stan said with his ribbed chest puffed out, giving off a false bravado.

"Just do it, Stan. I'm with Tyler. I'd rather not ruffle the old man's feathers."

Kelly could convince Stan to do anything. She was a year older than

106

both of us and her hourglass frame kept Stan wishing. We pretended not to notice, but our adolescent hormones refused to give an inch. But still, she was our best friend and we treated her like a sister.

As the jersey barrier came into view, so did Mr. Amesbury's faded yellow Victorian homestead. Luckily, the old man was nowhere in sight. His rocking chair on the front porch was empty. One thing did strike us as odd though: his small front lawn that was always meticulously maintained was overgrown with grass and weeds.

"See guys, we're cool. Old man's probably out grocery shopping or at the park looking to pick off a third grader for dinner tonight," Stan said, switching the radio back on. *Gettin' Jiggy Wit It* nearly blew out the speakers of Stan's hand-me-down boombox.

"Don't talk like that, Stan. The old man has had a rough enough life without more untrue rumors being spread around about him," I said.

"Hey, do you guys think it's true that he found his wife hanging in the basement by an extension cord?" Stan asked, clearly ignoring my request.

Kelly and I exchanged skeptical glances before our eyes shifted back to the only home on the street. Something felt off. Besides, the old man's rusty Oldsmobile was sitting in the driveway, *how far could he realistically get without it?*

"Just drop it," Kelly said.

Stan did just as she said.

As we passed by the graffitied plastic barriers, I looked back at the house, compelled by concern for the lonesome old timer. My heart jumped as I was caught off guard by a pair of glaring eyes that peeked out from a second story window. The reflection of trees on the windowpane made it tough to distinguish, but I knew it was Mr. Amesbury. He didn't yell, curse or wave his shotgun in the air. He just stared out the window. Despite the heat, a chill rolled down my back.

Heading down the trail, I decided to keep the eerie encounter to myself. Part of me didn't want to believe I actually saw what I saw and telling Kelly and Stan would all but confirm it was real.

Our day at the Basin was everything we hoped it would be. The crystal clear water was warm, and times were good as we splashed around. We laughed, sang along to the summer hits playing on the radio, and we'd all but forgotten Mr. Amesbury's mysterious absence. That is, until Kelly brought him up.

"So what do you guys think is up with Mr. Amesbury? I've never seen him leave his post. Especially not on days like this, when you could fry an egg on the sidewalk."

"Maybe he's finally given up. Got tired of kids ignoring his empty threats," Stan replied, his hands splashing against the surface of the water.

"No way, that's all that man has to live for. He's full of piss and vinegar and he *hates* kids with a passion," said Kelly.

Sitting on a rock with my legs hanging in the water, I skipped a flat stone across the water before I replied, trying to inject some empathy into the conversation. "I mean...can you really blame him? Poor guy lost everything in a freak accident. I'm honestly surprised he's hung out this long without punching his own time card."

"I don't feel bad at all. The guy needs to leave us alone and let us have fun," Stan said, again asserting his bravado.

"No...I get what Tyler is saying. We think he's just keeping us from having a good time, but maybe he's trying to protect us from what happened to his son," Kelly said, her tone softer.

"Exactly. I don't know. Maybe I've been in the sun too long, but I kind of pity the guy," I said, remembering what I'd seen earlier. Those eyes staring out the window longingly at us as we passed by his inefficient barrier.

"That's because you're a softy," Stan joked, splashing water up at me. Kelly reciprocated with a splash in my defense giving me time to stand up and return fire with a cannonball. We let the conversation about the old man fall away to the sound of *Semi-Charmed Life*. Summer was in full swing, and we were living it.

The next day, I called up the gang to see what was on the agenda. Stan was going fishing with his dad who only came around once every couple of months since his parents separated. Kelly was busy volunteering at the Boys and Girls club. I was on my own.

I'm not sure exactly, but something coerced me into mowing Mr. Amesbury's lawn. Maybe it was the cooler than average day, maybe it was the fear of boredom. Perhaps I was just a big softy like Stan said. Either way, here I was walking my dad's push mower down Beech Street towards the old Victorian on the left. I decided that if Mr. Amesbury were back on duty that I would just turn around and go back home, but he was nowhere in sight.

The grass appeared to have grown a foot taller than it was yesterday. I pushed the mower up to the edge of his driveway and paused to take a look around at a few of the windows. The car was still parked in the driveway and coated with a generous layer of pollen and dust. After raising up the mower deck a couple inches, I gave the pull cord a few rips. The mower fired up and I was off.

Lucky for me, the lawn was fairly small. I thought for sure Mr. Amesbury would come out to the porch at the sound of the mower, but he remained inside.

I couldn't help but feel a tinge of nervousness even though I was doing what I felt was a good deed. All my prior interactions with the old man had been less than pleasant, but something inside me knew he was just lonely.

After a few more passes, I looked up at the house with the eerie feeling of being watched. I was right. Mr. Amesbury was standing in the same window I'd spotted him in the day before. The same hollow expression on his face as he looked down at me.

My heartbeat accelerated and I wiped the sheen of sweat from my brow before offering an awkward smile and a wave. He acknowledged neither, turned away, and disappeared into the room. The previously occupied window only reflected the greens and blues of summer.

After I decided he had no intention of coming out to greet or berate me, I finished up with the lawn. The temperature only increased a little that afternoon, so I stuck around to pluck the accumulating weeds out of his flower beds and after finding a rickety old rake on the side of the porch I raked the piles of grass off the lawn. I'd considered topping off the job by watering his flowers that were wilting from thirst, but I couldn't find a hose. In hindsight, I was more than happy I couldn't find it because I hadn't been able to shake that feeling of being watched.

I returned the rake, admired my work for less than a minute, but didn't stick around long enough to pat myself on the back.

"See ya around, Mr. Amesbury," I called out to no one. Heading back home from Beech Street, the squeaky wheels of the mower reminded me I'd need to oil them later this afternoon like my father had asked. I don't know what it was, but a voice inside my head told me to turn around and go back. *Go back, knock on the door and make sure the old man's okay.* Instead, I looked back over my shoulder to see the silhouette of a man sitting in the rocking chair amidst the growing shadows of the afternoon. I couldn't make out who it was, but I was sure I knew.

§

The next morning, the smell of bacon and biscuits woke me from my sleep. I stretched my tight muscles, got dressed and went downstairs.

"Good morning, sweetheart. You sure slept in today," my mother greeted me with a plate. "I was just coming up to get ya."

"Yeah, I'm exhausted."

"Playing hard yesterday with the guys?" she said, seemingly forgetting Kelly was in fact a female.

"No, they were busy yesterday," I punctured the golden yolk of the egg with my fork debating whether to bring it up. "I actually went over to Mr. Amesbury's place and cleaned up his yard. I don't know what's going on over there, but his lawn was a disaster. The grass was up to my knees."

Nearly choking on her orange juice, she lowered her glass and asked, "You did what?" Her eyes told me she was equally surprised and concerned.

"It's no big deal. I just felt bad for the guy. He's all alone out there, and kids are always arguing with him. I thought it would be a sort of peace offering to help him out. Maybe he'll stop harassing us for just wanting to go swimming."

My mother cleared her throat and set her glass down on the table. "Well I don't think that's going to be a problem anymore, Tyler. I'm sorry to tell you but Mr. Amesbury was found dead inside his house over a week ago. The mailman noticed his mail piling up and called the cops. They did a wellness check and that's when they found him."

Suddenly, my appetite vanished, and I dropped my fork while a million questions raced through my head.

"What do you mean? What happened to him?" I asked, my voice trembling,. "I mean, how did he die?"

"I don't really think that's import—"

"Mom, please...how did he die? I'm not a kid anymore." The irony of my statement spoken with my cracking prepubescent voice lost amongst the seriousness of the conversation.

"Apparently, he was losing his battle with cancer and his insurance wouldn't cover anymore treatments. The police found the end of an old garden hose duct taped to his car's exhaust pipe sitting on the floor of his bedroom. He'd fed it in through the window, then sealed off any cracks and left his car running until it ran out of gas. By that time, he was dead."

I was at a loss for words.

"He was found lying in his bed. He'd been dead for a while. It's so awful. That poor guy."

My mother went on to talk about how she'd attended school with Scott and remembered how proud his parents were of all his achievements, but her words were drowned out by my thoughts: the visions of mean old Mr. Amesbury's eyes staring down at me the past few days.

Those sad eyes. Those dead eyes.

A TRAILER PARK CHRISTMAS

Like every other Christmas Eve, Carl sat alone in his mobile home. December was a festive time in the trailer park, but this year, Carl's lot looked abandoned. His was the only trailer without colorful lights hanging from the roof. No holly, jolly wreath adorned his screen door. The corner of his living room did not have the customary tree decorated with glass bulbs, tinsel, or lights. Not a single holiday card was displayed on his refrigerator—or anywhere else, for that matter. The only evidence of the holiday season was the Santa hats worn by the polar bears printed on the cans of Coke he was mixing with his whiskey.

Don't get it confused; Carl was no Ebenezer Scrooge by any means. He used to love the holiday season. In the years prior, he would have been the first to decorate his home. It had been a tradition since he was a young boy to put up the decorations the week after Thanksgiving, no matter how much it annoyed his parents. Now, he did all he could to avoid any reminders of Christmas, which was no easy task.

This Christmas Eve, he had passed out drunk in his faux leather recliner watching *M*A*S*H,* wearing only his torn work pants and a stained tank top. As the hour approached midnight, the cable network switched to *It's a Wonderful Life* to the sound of Carl's sawmill snoring. Had he been awake, he would have immediately changed the channel. Even on Christmas, he had no interest in watching Capra's classic film.

As George Bailey contemplated suicide on the 12" television screen, a heavy *thump* sounded on the metallic roof above. This was soon followed by tapping noises muffled by the snow that had accumulated there. It wasn't a tapping like somebody lightly banging a hammer, nor did it sound like the prancing of eight tiny reindeer that one might expect given the occasion. It sounded more like the pitter-patter of little feet. Several sets of little feet, to be exact.

Carl, oblivious in his drunken slumber, had a syrupy bead of spittle hanging from his drooping bottom lip. His smudged glasses rested in the patch of chest hair sprouting from beneath his tank top. They were attached to a strap around his neck so he wouldn't lose them.

Outside, the *thumping* of small boots landing in the snow could be heard from the porch situated beside the trailer.

On the television, a twelve-year-old George Bailey is rescuing his brother Harry from drowning in the frozen pond when somebody knocked hard on Carl's loosely hung screen door.

Carl snapped awake. "What the...?" His blurred eyes darted confusedly around the dimly lit room, unsure of what had woken him up. He rubbed his eyes, then clumsily placed his glasses onto the bridge of his nose. As he became more fully awake, he reached over to the stack of milk crates he used as an end table and grabbed his drink. Taking a swig to wet his whistle, he heard another knock on the front door.

Carl was so startled at the sudden pounding that he spilled his drink into his lap. "Shit! Goddamn it! Who the hell is knocking at this hour?" he barked as he peered up at the clock on the wall. Five past midnight. "Christ, that better be a beautiful, young hooker."

Carl leaned forward in the recliner and set down his drink. Standing up, he noticed the television was no longer playing his favorite show, but a Christmas movie instead. *Bleh!* He grabbed the remote control that was jammed into the side of the recliner cushion and quickly changed the channel.

He was oblivious to the pair of glowing green eyes peering in at him through the window, nor the tiny fingers clawing at the screen, eager to get inside.

The knock at the door came again, but this time it was more assertive.

"Jesus, hold your horses," he called. Then added under his breath, "Probably those damn kids from next door."

The floor settled under his weight as he walked to the door. His head spun wildly from the booze. The rundown trailer was a sufficient living space for himself, but he never meant for it to become his permanent home. Last month, he had been in talks with the bank about using his Christmas bonus for a down payment on a two-bedroom ranch the next town over. He was also up for a considerable promotion. Unfortunately, this fell through following the company owner's sudden death, along with his wife and two children. They were killed in a hit-and-run after leaving the annual company Christmas party the last week of November. All the workers in the plant had been laid off. Over 100+ people left jobless just weeks before Christmas. Carl was devastated.

So here he remained, in the West Burnchester trailer park. A jobless alcoholic with no family. His minuscule military pension helped pay the bills and stock up his liquor cabinet, but it wasn't enough to get him into a new home.

He sluggishly made it to the door and flipped on the porch light. Snow was steadily falling. The hexagonal window in the door gave off the illusion that he was flying through space. He stood on his tippy toes and peered outside to get a glimpse of the intruder but saw no one.

"Who's there? Do you know what time it is?" he said. No response came. Carl opened the door and swung it open, expecting to see some nosey kids waiting with snowballs, but no-one was there.

In the snow, he could see several small boot prints heading in all directions. Someone had torn the screen down the middle. He noticed small, greasy handprints had been pressed against the glass on the bottom half of the screen door. A cold draft of snow pushed its way through the torn screen, sending a chill down Carl's flesh. Shivering, he folded his arms across his chest.

"Son-of-a-bitch. Who the hell is out there?" he called out. "You show yourselves right now, you little pricks. I don't play games."

Poking his head through the door, he looked in all directions to see if he could spot anyone hiding in the shadows. Carl heard what sounded like the high-pitched laughter of children mixing with the whistle of the wind.

"I know you're out there. Shouldn't you be in bed waiting for Santy Claus, you little punks? Where are your parents?" Still, no response came.

He supposed the noise could have just been the wind blowing through the trees or the loose siding on the trailer, but something wasn't sitting right with him. Carl looked quizzically one more time at the small handprints, then slammed the door behind him.

"I'll be sure to call the landlord this morning. Christmas or no Christm–" Carl's words were cut off by the sound of breaking glass coming from the back of the trailer. A brisk wind howled through the broken window, bringing with it a gust of snow. "Are you fucking kidding me?"

He sounded infuriated, but the truth was, Carl was beginning to feel a little nervous. He wanted to believe it was kids just playing a prank on him, but this was getting out of hand.

After storming through the living room, he entered the kitchen. He eyed the 8-inch kitchen knife that rested by the sink and considered grabbing it. *It's just kids, Carl. Don't be foolish.* His thought was interrupted when he jammed his bad knee into a wooden chair beside the table. A surge of pain shot through his nervous system and sent him stumbling into the entrance to the hallway, hitting the wall hard with his shoulder.

Carl lost his breath and had to take a second to regain his composure. A sudden jingling sound caught his attention. He peered down the hallway in time to see something small dart by in the darkness. *Were those bells?* he thought, as he was now sure it was kids playing a Christmas prank on him. Too bad for them; he wasn't the playful type.

"Hey, kid! You better get the hell out of my trailer before I count to ten," he said, wincing in pain as he put weight on his injured leg. He placed a hand on the wallpapered paneling.

Through gritted teeth, the countdown began. "One. Two. Three." He started limping his way down the dark hallway. "You little shit... Better hope I don't get to ten."

He hobbled up to the first bedroom—mainly for used storage—and reached past the door frame to turn on the light. Nothing happened; then he remembered he'd forgotten to change the blown bulb. *Perfect,* he thought, then continued the countdown to Judgement Day.

"Four. Five. Six." His tone grew harsher with every number as the pain in his leg increased, "I'm warning you. I have a constitutionally protected right to defend my property."

He approached the door to the bathroom. His anger shifted to unease. *If this wasn't just some neighborhood kids playing a prank, what on earth could it be?* The wind continued to blow snow in through the broken backdoor window, which was forming a small snowdrift in the hallway. The frigid air sent another shiver down Carl's arms. *It's gonna cost me a fortune to fix that, sonsabitches,* he thought. A shimmer caught his attention on the broken. Thin strands of tinsel had caught on the broken shards of glass. *The hell?*

Flipping on the light to the bathroom, he was greeted by the bright glow of the halogen. He looked around. Nothing looked out of place. The shower curtain around the tub was pulled back, leaving nowhere for a kid to hide in the tiny room.

He turned towards the back room—his bedroom—and continued the countdown.

"Seven. Eight. You're cutting close. Last chance."

From the living room, he could hear an infomercial for a holiday CD playing samples of old Christmas tunes by generic pop artists.

Oh, the weather outside is frightful, but the fire is so delightful...

Carl looked toward the living room and let out an angry snarl. "I got your delightful right here," he said, grabbing his crotch.

Turning back to his bedroom, he pushed open the door a little bit. An unpleasant, high-pitched giggle—the sound of a child who also happened to be a heavy smoker—came from somewhere within the bedroom. He had them cornered; they had nowhere to go.

"Nine. You're fucked. You had your chance."

He reached in and turned on the light.

"Ten! Now you're mine!"

Elbowing the door, it swung open the rest of the way and slammed against his bed frame. His hand was still resting on the light switch. Over his bed, he saw words crudely carved into the paneling.

§

When justice is done, it brings joy to the righteous
but terror to THE NAUGHTY.

§

"What the fuck? COME OUT NO—" His words were cut off by a searing surge of pain as the bones on his right hand were crushed by a blunt force. Carl let out a scream of agony as he pulled his hand back to look at it. Gripping his wrist below the wound, he saw it wasn't crushed, but something had pierced the center of his hand. Whatever it was had left a hole two-inches diameter straight through his hand. He could see the floor through the gore and pieces of broken bone protruding from the hole. The pain was unbearable. He looked down to see his attacker and wished he hadn't.

A short figure draped in a dark green hooded robe stood knee-high about two feet away from Carl. It wore scuffed black boots with sharp metal spikes jutting from each toe. It was about the size of a child, but the facial features and wrinkled hands said otherwise. It pulled back the hood and rested it on its shoulders. Carl watched in horror as the thing licked the blood off the pointed end of the large candy cane it had used to puncture his hand. Its tongue slipped out between red, cracked lips that were enwreathed by a long, graying beard. Carl noticed it had pointed ears, except one of them looked as though something had bitten off half of it. Dangling from the ear lobes were earrings—strands of hair threaded through dangling human eyeballs.

Carl was in shock and disbelief at what stood before him, but the immense pain in his hand reassured him that it was all very real.

He opened his mouth to speak but stopped as another small, hooded creature rose from behind his bed. It held out defensively a set of sharpened reindeer antlers while it growled at Carl from the other side of the bed. This one looked more corroded, with pale green skin. Around its neck, it wore a necklace adorned with severed ears. The nose was a plump purple thing

118

covered in reddish spider veins. The rest of the attire matched that of its comrade.

Carl could hear someone on the television was singing, "*Let it snow, let it snow, let it snow.*"

"What is this? You some sort of demented gang? Look at my fucking hand!" Carl tried to sound angry, but fear was creeping into his voice. Speaking louder, he said, "Is this a robbery? Well, I don't have shit to steal, you jackasses. Look at me. I'm broke as a joke!" His words trembled as the pain in his hand shot up, making him weak in the knees.

The wicked pair just watched the man in the tank top stand there, blood running down his arm and onto the floor while he desperately pleaded for answers. They shot each other crooked smiles, flashing their jagged, rotten teeth, as if they relished his pain and suffering. The first one took another lick of the grotesque candy cane, savoring the taste of Carl's blood. The second one licked its lips, enticed by the pooling blood.

Carl's rage left him. Now he looked scared and despondent. There was no way he'd be able to outrun them with his injured knee.

His life was miserable and hopeless, but he didn't want to die. Not like this.

"*What do you want?*" he screamed. "Do you want me to beg? Is that what you want?"

The intruder took another lick, unbothered by the pathetic sight Carl presented.

Carl gave in. Using his good hand, he leaned against the doorframe and slowly lowered himself onto his aching knee. The pair approached him with menacing expressions, clearly not here to grant clemency.

Carl's eyes welled up as he began his plea for mercy. "Please, I beg you. Don't kill me. I want to live." This triggered no emotional response from the two, angering Carl. "*Please!* For God sakes, *it's Christmas—*"

His cries were cut short when a small, rough hand gripping his sweaty forehead and yanked his head backward. He felt pressure on his calf muscles as little boots stepped up onto his legs. A second hand swung around the other side and began to shove something into Carl's gaping mouth. Carl looked across the room at the standing mirror against the wall and caught a brief glimpse of what he was choking on: small, black cubes of coal. The taste was awful. He sucked in bits of dust, and loose pieces broke off as he desperately gasped for breath.

Please make it quick. Just let it be over with, Carl thought, hoping God would be listening. Some part of him worried it was far from over.

The two intruders joined their accomplice, bells jingled with each footfall.

Tears escaped from Carl's bloodshot eyes as a snippet of "Silent Night" played on the television. It reminded him of when his grandparents would bring him to church on Christmas Eve. He'd always loved the hymns.

Carl nearly forgot about the pain until the third intruder clobbered him on the base of his skull. Pain flared for a moment, then the world around Carl went dark.

§

Carl woke to find himself driving his car down a snowy road.

This was a dream. No—a nightmare.

The telephone poles were decorated with Christmas wreaths, and the trees were glistening with beautiful white lights through the freshly fallen snow. His head was heavy with drunkenness from the numerous drinks he'd had that night to celebrate his promotion. He knew he shouldn't be driving, but he didn't have any friends to stop him.

He tapped his hands on the steering wheel to the beat of an old-time Christmas song he'd always loved. As he approached a red light, his attention was pulled away by a Christmas display that decorated the front lawn of a beautiful two-story house. I'll own a house like that soon enough. It's what I deserve, he boasted to himself.

The lights made him feel nostalgic, and he got lost in the past. He remembered visiting his grandparent's at Christmastime and the warm feeling of sitting by the fire in front of the tree.

Carl blew through the red light and reality came crashing back when he clipped the rear end of a passing car, sending the other car into a tailspin, its tires skating over the icy road, out of control.

Carl slammed on his brakes and managed to skid to a stop and avoid slamming into a telephone pole. His head was spinning crazily as he rolled down his window to see what he'd hit. There was nothing in sight. He rubbed his eyes, unbuckled his belt, and stepped out into the snow.

Once out of the car, a jolt of pain shot up from his right knee. He was so intoxicated, he hadn't felt it jam into the underside of the dashboard. Limping, he returned to the point of collision and noticed a second pair of tire tracks. He followed them with his eyes until he spotted a gap in the guard rail.

He made his way over and peered down into the deep gulley below. What looked like a car had flipped onto its roof after smashing into several trees on its way down. From what he could see, nobody had crawled from the overturned vehicle. The falling snow softly landed on the exposed undercarriage of the car, melting as it touched the hot piping of the exhaust.

Carl was overcome with guilt. He fought the urge to vomit as he looked down at the car. The car he'd driven off the road and the people he possibly killed.

His entire future flashed before his eyes, and in an instant, he knew what he had to do. He glanced around at the roads and nearby homes and saw no witnesses.

Run, a voice in his mind told him, get out of here.

Carl stumbled back to his car, trying to ignore the pain in his knee, and drove home as carefully as he could. He hoped to make a clean escape and put this all behind him. For a while, he'd thought he'd done just that since the police never called him in for questioning.

§

He opened his eyes. It had just been a dream. He lay there for a moment in a state of confusion. He was in pain, and he was cold, and it helped to clear his thoughts. He was laying in the snow, staring up at the night sky. Snow was still falling. His jaw ached, and he gagged as he tried to take a breath. He lifted his hand to feel what was crammed into his mouth, and his palm erupted with pain.

It all came back to him. He had been home. It was Christmas morning. Someone had broken into his house. *There were three intruders,* he recollected, slipping into a state of panic, *little demonic things.*

The intruder holding the antlers kicked wet snow into Carl's face, and he shot up into a sitting position.

"Merry Christmas, murderer," a deep voice boomed from somewhere in the darkness. Puffs of breath escaped the darkness from whoever was speaking. One of the intruders hocked a loogie onto Carl's face. The thick wad of snot ran down his bristly cheek, but he didn't dare wipe it off.

Carl could not speak. His mouth was still full of coal. He struggled to breathe through his nose as he painstakingly followed the order.

I'm not a murderer, he thought, now on the verge of tears. *I'm not a murderer. It was just a bad dream.* He noticed all three intruders standing in front of him, the snow up to their thighs.

"I said, get on your knees!" the voice demanded. Carl squinted but could not see who was there.

Fighting through the pain, he did as he was told, afraid of the repercussions if he disobeyed. Finally on his knees, he settled into the snow.

Two of the intruders turned to face each other and bowed their heads.

A looming figure at least a foot or two taller than Carl stepped from the darkness and into the light of a streetlamp. As wide as a refrigerator, it wore a black hooded cloak trimmed with what appeared to be human. The snow seemed to avoid the figure, blowing around but never settling on its large frame. It was as if its body was emanating an intense amount of heat. Thick steam rose off the cloak before dissipating into the air. Carl noticed as the figure took heavy steps forward that the snow around its boots sizzled and melted into a black puddle, staining the snow around it. Carl couldn't see it clearly, but the figure was dragging a heavy wooden object.

It stopped a few feet in front of Carl and paused. Tears streamed from Carl's eyes. Whatever he had done to deserve this meeting, he was now sorrier than ever.

With its free hand, the figure pushed back the heavy hood, revealing a man's face. He was practically bald. A fringe of black hair encircled his bare scalp and flowed down over his impossibly broad shoulders, and he sported a thick, bushy, black beard.

The man belted out a mock laugh, sounding like a lewd Santa Claus. "You've been naughty, Carl. *Very, very* naughty."

Carl knelt in terrified awe, unable to speak a word.

The man spoke as if he was a father scolding his child, his voice reverberating into the night like distant thunder.

"You are one of the wretched few who was naughty enough to make my list," he explained, patting at his breast. The minions all hissed the word *naughty* at the mention of the list.

"Do you know who stands before you?" he asked, knowing Carl couldn't answer.

Carl violently shook his head.

"All you gluttonous, greedy humans know of jolly, old Saint Nick. My dollar-store whore of a brother." The three minions chuckled. "All because you believe he brings you presents and candy and all those material things you ask for. Garbage is what I call it." Spitting into the snow, it sizzled as it made contact. "Nobody knows of his younger sibling. That is until—as is in your case—it is too late. Carl Scottsdale, you are in the presence of Dominicus Claus, the Bringer of Christmas Judgement. I have not brought you presents on this Christmas morning. No candy. No; I have come to take something from you. Something that is rightfully mine." Dominicus's face lit up with a smile so wide his jagged, stained teeth were visible. "Your meaningless life."

Carl's eyes grew wide as a tightness balled up in his chest.

"They," Dominicus waved a hand towards the minions, "are my most loyal servants. There are many of them, but tonight, there are three. Think of them as the Three Wise Men if it brings you comfort."

Dominicus continued his monologue. "They were once Santa's elves, slaving away in his sweatshops for hours on end. Making toys for all the little boys and girls who didn't do *anything* to deserve them. That is, until my brother cast them out for having the balls to question his authority. You see, my brother is a bit of an authoritarian. Control over others is what truly brings him joy. What truly makes him...jolly. He thrives on the fact that he alone gets to pick which kids get presents and which get *nothing.*" Dominicus growled the last word.

One of the elves let out a gravelly hiss through its gritted teeth and bounced his sharpened candy cane into his open palm.

"Now they humbly serve the one-and-only anti-Christmas. The yin to Santa's yang. Serving up the naughtiest of naughties on a platter to their beloved. Yours truly."

The elves chanted *naughty, naughty* in a taunting, schoolyard fashion.

"But enough of this," Dominicus roared, sounding indignant. The elves stopped their chants. "Now that I have enlightened you as to who we are, sentencing shall commence."

Carl mistakenly gulped, swallowing more bits of coal, and winced in pain.

Dominicus moved a step closer. Steam rose from the snow around his large boot. Reaching into his robe, he pulled out a large scroll, unrolled it, and began to read the text.

"*You*, Carl E. Scottsdale, are responsible for the untimely death of the Bartlett family. A loving mother, a supportive father, and their two innocent children. All of them died because you had one too many drinks. *You* drove them off the road. *You* ran home like a dog with its tail between its legs. *You* didn't even check to see if they were alive. Didn't look in the rearview mirror. Didn't even call for help." His judgmental voice now echoed like they were inside a cathedral.

The three elves growled as they slowly backed away from Carl, preparing for the oncoming judgment.

Suddenly, it all became clear to Carl what this was all about. What the dream was about. It was no dream. He had killed his boss and his family. He was responsible for all his friends losing their jobs. Carl was overwhelmed by long-overdue remorse, knowing that, as impossible as it seemed, this was all really happening.

It was time to meet his maker, and he deserved no mercy.

Time as he knew it slowed. All around him, there was nothing but silence.

Dominicus Claus, Bringer of Christmas Judgement, lifted the wooden object he held in his huge hand. Carl tried to gasp as he saw the head of a mallet rise up out of the snow. Chunks of coal were wedged deeply down his esophagus, and he choked. It all made sense. It wasn't just a mallet; it was an enormous gavel. On the rounded end of the gavel, he could make out stains of dried blood mixed with chunks of flesh and broken bits of bone.

Time sped back up in time for Carl to hear Dominicus bellow out as he lifted the gavel high over his head, "When justice is done, it brings joy to the righteous but terror to the naughty. Peace be to the dead. Judgment to the sinner."

Carl took his last breath and closed his eyes. *I'm sorry*, he thought with self-pity. Sorry for those he'd unintentionally killed, but mostly for himself.

Dominicus brought down the gavel with all his might on top of Carl's skull. His head disintegrated in a spray of blood and gore while his collarbone collapsed in on itself. It sounded like somebody smashing a pumpkin. The crimson mixture of blood and brain matter sprayed out in all directions like a macabre tie-dye on the white snow. The elves cheered as they were showered in Carl's blood. They stuck out their tongues to catch the spray like children catching snowflakes. Carl's body continued to collapse under the weight of the blow.

The elves wasted no time cleaning up the mess they'd made. It was their favorite part of the job, after all. They walked over to what remained of Carl and collected what parts they could find. They made their way back to the trailer, sneaking a nibble or two along the way. Climbing the stairs to the porch, they tossed the carcass onto the living room floor like a bag of trash.

Another infomercial was playing during the commercial break.

Dominicus made his way up to the porch. The wooden stairs nearly gave out under the weight of his gigantic body. He bit off the end of a large cigar, then, with a snap of his finger, lit the tip while admiring his work. He walked up to the door with his gavel resting on his shoulder. Cigar smoke billowed around his head like a halo. Peering in at Carl one last time, he paused. A song on the television caught his attention: *Here comes Santa Claus, here comes Santa Claus, right down Santa Claus Lane...* The upbeat Christmas tune celebrating his brother spilled from the TV's speakers. Dominicus flashed it a look of disgust.

"I fucking hate that song," he jeered, flicking the lit cigar onto the carpet. With a wave of his hand, the floor lit up like the 4th of July. Flames climbed up the curtains, spread to the ceiling, and swallowed the recliner. Carl's body was engulfed in violent fire. Within minutes, the rest of the trailer was ablaze, lighting up the trailer park.

The elves applauded from the lawn as they watched the roof slowly collapsing in on itself. Dominicus set down his gavel, clapped his massive hands, smiling. In a way, he looked almost jolly. The fire reflected in his dark eyes, making them twinkle.

"Let's go, boys," he called to the elves. They scrambled up onto the porch one by one, and without hesitation, their bells jingling merrily, they jumped into the blaze. Dominicus Claus, the Bringer of Christmas Judgement, took one last look around. He removed the *Naughty List* and a quill pen from his breast pocket. Dipping the quill in the blood coating the head of his gavel, he scratched out the name ~~Carl Edmund Scottsdale~~ before returning the items to his pocket. Finally, he followed the elves into the fire, where the four of them vanished without a trace.

Their work was complete. Justice was done.

That is, until next Christmas.

MAN OF MY DREAMS

It was the same every night, Ainsley and Cara would lie in bed side-by-side—Cara quietly reading her true crime paperback for no longer than 15 minutes before falling asleep with the book resting across her chest, and Ainsley fading off into one of her favorite sitcoms while working on a crossword puzzle. Once she started to get tired, she would set the sleep timer on the television, roll over and go to sleep.

The television screen would flicker hues of light across the comforter and onto the sleeping couple. Cara hated having television on while they slept but she knew it helped her wife fall asleep sooner, so she didn't complain. Besides, she never set the sleep timer for longer than one hour, giving her ample time to doze off before the room fell into total darkness.

It's not that Ainsley was necessarily afraid of the dark, but she *was* afraid of her dreams. Since she was a little girl, she'd struggled with lucid dreaming. She loved to talk about her dreams, if and when they were happy. Sometimes they were even fun. She could visit her childhood hangouts and friends, spend time with dead relatives and pets, revisit past events in her life and have a redo as she liked to refer to it. Of course they were all just dreams. They had no real effect on the real world. Those that were dead were still dead. That embarrassing or mean thing she said still happened. But they felt real.

One might ask why she's afraid of her dreams if they're so interesting and interactive, but those are just the good dreams. She also struggled with extremely vivid nightmares. The ones she didn't like to tell Cara about over their morning coffee and tea. They were far too scary.

The trouble started shortly after the couple were married. Cara noticed something odd about her wife; for no reason at all, Ainsley would wake up screaming in the middle of the night. This would wake Cara from her deep sleep, confused and alarmed by the sudden commotion. Ainsley apologized and told her she had a bad dream, but that was it. No matter how often it happened, it was always 'just a bad dream,' and the two would go back to sleep.

Any attempt by Cara to pry for further explanation always led to an argument. Ainsley flat-out refused to elaborate on why she woke up screaming bloody murder, regardless of how much strain it was putting on their relationship.

That all changed one day in autumn when the couple invited over their friends Chris and Tanna for a few drinks by the bonfire.

The conversation mostly centered on horror movies, current political climate, and literature, but it swiftly took a turn towards existentialism and dreaming when Cara took the initiative to bring up Ainsley's more lucid dreaming.

"So let me get this straight, you are able to visit with Scampers from time to time even though he's been dead for 15 years?" Tanna asked, referring to Ainsley's tabby cat from high school.

"Quite often, in fact. It's funny because he will just pop up randomly in places that he had never been. Like that time we went to Funtown. For some reason, I dream of that place a lot. Anyway, one dream I was riding the roller coaster and in the middle of the ride Scampers came out of nowhere and jumped into my lap. The coaster was twisting and turning, he just sat in my lap, purring as he always did. Totally unaffected by the shifts in gravity. It's kind of funny, right?"

Cara listened, running her finger along the rim of her wine glass.

"I miss that cat. He would always greet me at the door when I'd come over. Rubbing his face on my calf," Tanna said. She looked over at Chris who was gazing lazily into the fire. "Are we boring you, Chris?" she asked, playfully slapping him on the arm.

"No, no. Not at all," was his reply.

"Yeah, he was a good cat. Dreams are so bizarre. It's almost like they're gateways to your past life. Or *lives*," Ainsley said.

"Oh I totally know what you mean," Cara replied, "mine aren't as vivid as yours, nor are they nearly as scary."

Ainsley shot her wife an angry yet quizzical look, as if she knew where this conversation was headed, and she less than appreciated it.

"Scary? How are dreams about your cat scary?" Tanna inquired, taking a sip of her IPA.

"Well..." she paused, looking at Cara with a less-than-impressed expression. "Those dreams aren't scary at all. But sometimes I have nightmares. You know, like everyone else. It's no big deal."

Influenced by her mojito-induced courage, Cara decided to take it a step further. She knew she was pushing the limits, but she assumed Ainsley would keep her cool around her best friend.

"Like everyone else? Psssh... Does everyone else wake up screaming at the top of their lungs? Do *you*, Tanna? Chris? Do you ever wake up from a dead sleep screaming like you've just been stabbed?"

"Nope. Can't say that I do," Chris spoke up from his can of domestic beer, the fire light sent ripples of orange across his clean-shaven face.

"Cara! That's not—" Ainsley started.

"Is that true, Ains? You wake up screaming?" Tanna asked, her tone moving away from inquisition to one of concern.

"Well—," Ainsley started again, before Cara cut her off.

"Oh big time. Wakes me up damn near every night. It really fucks with my sleep. I ask her about it, but she never wants to talk about it. Do ya, hon?"

"Cara. I don't appreciate—"

"Is it him?" Tanna asks, cutting off Ainsley's attempt to reprimand her wife.

Ainsley paused, shot Cara a cold expression, and looked at Tanna, "What?"

"I asked if it's *him*?" Tanna asked, anxiously scraping the label off her bottle of beer. "Do you see *him* in these nightmares?"

Ainsley stared into the fire as if she'd been betrayed. Clearly the drinks were having an adverse effect on the integrity of everyone she cared so deeply about tonight. 'Everyone,' just so happened to be her wife, and best friend, with whom she'd had an unspoken agreement to never bring up the nightmares or... *him* among other people. A trifecta of secrets with Ainsley was their catalyst. Cara knew nothing about *him,* and Tanna knew nothing about the nightmares. In these relationships built on trust, who was really being betrayed here?

"We are *not* going to talk about that tonight. You both have obviously had a bit too much to drink and this is not going to turn into some intoxicated therapy session. End—of—story," Ainsley declared, her eyes moved to the glowing embers pulsating in the fire.

The red wine was sending warm jolts of misguided confidence through Cara as she decided to further inquire about the mysterious *him.*

"Who are you talking about, Tanna?"

"She's talking about nobody! I don't want to talk about it."

"Sorry, Cara. I should have never brought it up." Tanna said, with a hint of shame in her tone. She realized she'd messed up.

Chris let out a loud and obnoxious belch, seemingly breaking the tension. All three of the women looked over at him with disgust then started to laugh.

"Is that all you have to say, Chris?" Tanna joked.

The laughter died down and they all watched the fire, sipping their lukewarm beverages. Shadows danced all around them as a cool breeze stoked the blaze.

"It's my father," Ainsley said, pulling her confession out of thin air.

The group looked over at her, but her eyes never left the fire.

"What's that, hon?" asked Cara.

"The man in my dreams. He's my father. It started when I was around 18, around the time you and I met," she said, pointing her mojito at Cara.

"But wait, didn't he die just before we met?" asked Cara.

"No. He died after we met, after things started getting serious between us."

Tanna took a swig of her beer, sensing that the conversation was about to get tense. Truths were about to be revealed and it was her fault.

"I know that's what I said, but that's not what actually happened."

"So wait, you lied to me?" Cara's anger was palpable, but Ainsley kept her cool.

"Babe, you don't know the whole story and for that I'm sorry. I should have told you sooner," Ainsley reached down, picked up the bottle of cabernet, and topped off her wife's glass. "Please, don't be mad. Just listen."

"My dad was old fashioned, and Catholic to boot. He was also strict. Wouldn't let me go out with friends. Wouldn't let me play sports. The only reason I ever got to see Tanna was because we were neighbors, and our fathers were buddies. Well, you can imagine that when I was getting ready to leave for university, he wanted to know all the details. That's around the time you and I met in lit class. I was going back and forth between the dorm and my parent's house, so my folks allowed me to keep Scampers at their place. Anyways, my parents decided to stop by the campus for a surprise visit one day, but they never made it to my dorm. Apparently they were walking through the courtyard when they spotted me at a picnic table. My back was to them, but they would have recognized my long red hair anywhere. You were sitting across from me and that's when they saw us holding hands. My dad lost his mind and my mom tried, but to no avail she couldn't calm him down. He just turned around and went home," Ainsley's voice began to quiver.

"The following weekend I went home for Thanksgiving break—which is when I'd planned to break the news to them that I was seeing someone. When I got home, no one was there, or so I thought. I went up to my room to put my clothes away and that's when I found him. Scampers. He was stretched out on my bed like he was sleeping. His belly had been cut open and his guts were splayed across my comforter. I fell to the floor. I screamed. I cried. I mourned for my friend. That's when I heard the maniacal laughter and noticed my father. He was standing up against the wall in the corner of the room. I'll never forget what he said to me that day. 'You fucking bitch. You lousy, stupid fucking bitch. After all we've done to provide for you. You decide to run off with some cunt. Who the fuck do you think you arc,' was

131

what he said to me. I asked him what he did to Scampers and he acted like he couldn't even hear me. 'You're an embarrassment and an abomination. Playing kissy face with a WOMAN? How could you betray your family like that?' I'll never forget the sheer hatred and disgust in his tone. I ignored his bigoted sermon and demanded an answer.

"'I asked you what you did to Scampers, you asshole!' That's when he drew the kitchen knife from his belt loop and charged at me," Cara shifted in her seat and Tanna sat upright, waiting for the reveal. She'd heard it all before.

"I ran out of my bedroom and down the stairs. My father must have forgotten about his bad knee in his rage because he tripped a few steps down from the top and tumbled the rest of the way. When he landed at my feet on the first floor, the steak knife was sticking out of his neck. He died , but not before he uttered the words, 'This isn't over, bitch.' Really nice, huh?"

"Jesus-fucking-Christ, Ains! How come you never told me this?" All her anger had dissolved, and all Cara had left to offer was empathy.

"Because, I didn't want you thinking it was your fault that he died. He had no right to be so angry. I fucking hated him in that moment, and I was happy he died."

"Ainsley? You don't mean that." Cara said.

"I absolutely mean that."

"I'm still mad about Scampers. He was the best fucking cat ever. Remember that time he brought in a baby mouse and left it on the couch, and your mom almost sat on it," Tanna said, attempting to lighten the mood.

"Wait a minute...You've been holding onto this secret for over fifteen years? Tanna knew this whole time, but you never told your wife," Cara's agitation returned with a vengeance.

"It's not like that, Ca—"

Cara cut off Tanna's attempt to keep the peace. "It most certainly is like that," Cara said, dumping out the rest of her half-filled glass of wine. "I've heard about enough from this 'intoxicated therapy session.'"

"Babe, please...I haven't told—"

"Goodnight to our esteemed guests. I hope you appreciate the fact that you know more about my own wife than I do." Cara stormed off, leaving the others in an awkward silence around the fire.

"Well, this has certainly been an enchanting evening," Chris said, before chugging the remainder of his beer.

"Shut up, jackass," Tanna scoffed, "are you going to tell her about the nightmares?"

Ainsley downed the rest of her mojito, "Do I really have a choice?"

§

Tanna and Chris went home. Chris being the functioning alcoholic of the couple drove them. Tanna felt like shit. She'd completely ruined the evening by bringing up the nightmares, even though she had no idea that Ainsley kept this secret from her wife. She didn't blame her, but that didn't make her feel any less guilty.

Back in the house, Ainsley slid into her pajamas while Cara sat quietly reading her copy of *The Orient Express*.

"I'm sorry," Ainsley started, knowing an apology was the safest way to win back her wife's trust. "I'm sorry I've kept this from you for so long. The fact is, I know how sensitive you are. I didn't want you taking responsibility for my father's death, because it wasn't like that at all. He brought that on himself. He was my father, but he was also a bigot. He couldn't accept the fact that I was in love and that you were a woman. That's on him. Not you... or me."

Cara slid her bookmark into place and set the novel on her nightstand. She looked into her wife's eyes, not with rage or disappointment, but empathy.

"I know. You're right. I probably would have broken up with you had I known that your dad was so upset. I don't know. I guess it just hurt that Tanna knew about it and I didn't."

"I know, babe. I'm sorry. I swear, that's the only secret I've ever kept from you. I love you more than anything. My dad was a sick man and if you had left me over him, I would have completely lost it. It was bad enough what he did to Scampers. Bastard was lucky he landed on the knife. I might've killed him myself."

"Oh come on, Ains. We don't need to hash up those terrible old memories. You're an amazing person and you're in a committed, loving marriage with a woman that adores you. He can't take that away from you," Cara said, smiling softly. "Say, you think maybe holding onto that secret for so long was what was giving you nightmares? Sometimes guilt can have bizarre effects on people."

"I don't know. Maybe you're right. It would be amazing to get a good night's sleep without worrying about waking you up with one of my nightmares."

"Well, let's see. It's getting late and I gotta get up early. We have a signing tomorrow and I need to set up the chairs and tables before the library opens."

Ainsley crawled into bed beside her wife. She leaned over and gently kissed Cara on the lips. Nose to nose she looked into Cara's eyes lustfully, "You're the best thing that's ever happened to me, Cara Margaret."

"Ewww—Don't say my middle name," Cara scoffed, playfully pushing Ainsley away before pulling her back a second later. "I love you, Ains. Now get some rest okay, babes?" She gave her a soft peck on the lips, fell back onto her pillow, and turned off her bedside lamp.

"I love you too. Hey, do you mind if I watch a little TV to tire myself out?"

"Of course not. Goodnight, love."

Cara rolled over and within minutes, was sleeping soundly.

Ainsley was stretched out. She laid with her head on the pillow, watching one of her late shows at low volume. She felt good about getting such a weight lifted on her shoulders. She felt even better that Cara was so understanding and in the end forgave her for keeping such a dark secret from her. She looked over at Cara. Her deep breaths and the way her long dark hair draped across her back gave her the urge to crawl up against her and snuggle, but she didn't want to disrupt her sleep.

It wasn't long into her show that Ainsley's eyelids grew heavy, and she began to doze off. She set the sleep timer for thirty minutes and let herself fall asleep.

§

Ainsley knew immediately after falling asleep that she'd landed directly into one of her nightmares. *She was back at her parent's house, but neither of them were there. She walked inside and was surprised to see Scampers perched on the couch. He didn't run to greet her like he normally would. Instead, he slowly made his way down off the couch. The smell hit Ainsley instantly and she retracted.*

"Hey, little buddy... I've missed you so much, Scamps." She bent down to pick him up as he approached. "Why're you so stinky, boy?" She placed her hands under his belly to lift him up and felt the opened cavity that had once been his soft pink tummy. Her hand slipped into his open gash making an awful wet sound. She dropped him, pulling her hands away and he scampered off into the house, a trail of blood spilling from his incision. Her hands were coated in thick congealed blood.

"Jesus Christ, what the fuck, Scampers? What the fuck?" Her heart was racing, she pounded up the stairs to the second story bathroom to wash the blood and gore from her hands and beneath her fingernails. She was shaking. She knew she was dreaming but it felt so real. So horrible.

Drying her hands with a towel, she felt lightheaded and suddenly wanted to lay down. Opening the door to her bedroom, she was hit with the odor of raw meat and iron. She swung open the door and screamed at the sight before her.

Cara was lying on her bed covered in dozens of knife wounds. Her eyes were open and her mouth agape, as though she'd tried to scream as she was stabbed.

"I told you, you stupid fucking bitch. I told you, this isn't over."

Her father stepped out of the dark corner, carrying the kitchen knife. The gaping hole in his neck was spurting blood with every step. "You're going to pay for betraying your mother and me. You're an abomination. A stain. A sinner."

"FUCK YOU! YOU'RE DEAD!"

He ran at her at full speed with the knife raised and brought it down just above her right breast. The jolt of pain shot down her body and she screamed.

"AAAAAHHHHH!"

§

Ainsley shot up in bed. The room was pitch black, and she looked around frantically for her father, but she couldn't see him anywhere in the room. She reached over and felt for Cara. Her hand found Cara's head and she was thankful she hadn't woken her.

"God... it felt so real. So real," she whispered, running her hands through her hair and wiping the sweat from her forehead. She looked at the alarm clock which read 12:53am. "Phew. I can still try and get some sleep," she leaned over and kissed Cara on the head, fell back onto her pillow, and after a while back to sleep.

§

Ainsley woke up early and decided to sneak out of the bedroom to fix Cara a nice breakfast before she left for work. She felt so much better having come clean last night and regardless of her terrible nightmare, she wanted to show Cara how much she loved her. Things were going to be different from now on. No more secrets. No more guilty conscience. She wouldn't let her father win. He was long gone, and she had her whole life ahead of her with Cara. *She* won.

Placing a pair of perfectly cooked over-easy eggs onto a plate beside the crispy bacon and whole wheat toast (Cara's favorite breakfast), she set it on the table beside a glass of orange juice.

"Cara? Are you awake, babe? I got a surprise for you," she called. She listened for footsteps but heard nothing. "Cara? You have to get ready for work, hon. Poor girl, that third glass of wine really did a number on her," she said to herself.

She adjusted the placement of the silverware one last time then walked to the bedroom. Ainsley knocked gently at first before quietly pushing it open. The morning sunshine poured over the dark bedroom and Ainsley could see Cara still lying in bed. Her gorgeous dark hair spilling over her shoulders and pillow. She walked around the bed to wake her wife with a good morning kiss.

Ainsley placed her hand on Cara's bare shoulder, leaned in, and gave her a kiss on the forehead. She felt cold, "Hey babe, it's time to get up. Are you feeling okay? You feel really cool." Cara was always a warm sleeper, something wasn't right. "Cara, stop messing around. I made you some breakfast. You gotta get ready for work. Remember, the book signing? Ralph will kill you if—" Ainsley pulled back the blankets, making a sticky wet sound. Ainsley stood there, afraid to move, "Cara? Did you puke, baby? Come on, I'll get you in the shower. It's no big deal."

Ainsley reached down to the night stand and flicked on the lamp. She gasped and fell back onto the floor, her back slammed against the wall. Cara was covered in blood that had seeped out of a dozen or more stab wounds. Ainsley began to hyperventilate, and her eyes filled with tears.

"NOOOO! CARA!"

On the wall behind their bed was a message, written in blood, just six bold letters.

S-I-N-N-E-R.

The eye was dotted with a kitchen knife. *The* kitchen knife.

In the back of her mind, Ainsley could hear the last words her father ever spoke to her: 'This isn't over, bitch.'

This time, there were two extra words.

'I WON.'

DESECRATED

The bodies were never supposed to be found, but that which has been desecrated can't stay hidden forever. That's a lesson I'll never forget.

It all started on a warm and sunny afternoon in June when I signed my grandfather out from ward 7C so we could do our monthly fishing excursion. He was always so happy to see me. Frankly, I couldn't blame him. The smells coming out of that ward were less than pleasant.

I always loved to see the smile on his face as he came rolling down the hallway on his motorized wheelchair. I'd pretend not to see the gangrenous sores on the backs of his legs or the way his legs bent further inward with each passing month. I wanted to remember my grandfather the way I'd known him as a kid. The man who would bring me to the county fair, taught me to swim and ride a bicycle, and of course, our early afternoon fishing trips. To be honest, seeing him in this condition frightened me. I was scared of getting old. Scared of withering away in a hospital bed hoping someone would visit me. Scared to die.

On our walk through building 207 to the main entrance, he would ask me about my life, how school was going, if I'd found myself a little lady friend yet. Same old, same old. It was nice to have someone so interested in my life. I could tell he genuinely cared and wasn't just filling the void with meaningless conversation. Truth is, I liked my visits with Grandpa.

As we passed through the automatic doors and stepped out into the fresh air, Grandpa stopped to inhale deeply. It must have been such a relief to be free of that ward and its odor of sickness and death, even if it was just for a couple of hours.

I started to turn right to head towards our usual fishing spot just west of the East Cemetery, but Grandpa grabbed me by the wrist and said he would rather to head up towards the pond just before the north entrance of the hospital grounds. I explained that fishing was prohibited in that pond, but he scoffed and swatted a hand at me as if to say *pish tosh*.

Heading down the sloping sidewalk, we saw a young man busy at work mowing the lawn. He was wearing headphones and sunglasses but when he noticed us he flashed us a friendly wave.

After stopping by the parking lot so I could grab my poles and tackle box from my truck, we made our way to the pond. Luckily, there weren't any VA police in sight to harass us about fishing where we weren't allowed, which helped me relax a little bit.

The flowers of late spring shivered in the gentle breeze that accompanied the chorus of songbirds. Rays of warm afternoon sunshine poked through the lush green foliage of the surrounding maples.

The gentle *plop* of the first worm hitting the surface of the water was a far more potent anti-depressant than any pill the psychiatrist could have prescribed for Grandpa. The ripples danced outward away from the red and white bobber. Grandpa leaned forward in his wheelchair, looking to be ten years younger than he had in the ward. This was his happy place and in all honesty, it was mine too.

After Grandpa settled in with his pole, I threaded a fat nightcrawler onto my hook and cast my line. *Plop*. We didn't talk much when we fished. It was an unspoken rule that when lines were in the water, our mouths stayed closed. I never thought of him as a superstitious man, but he was certainly big on tradition.

"Whoop! Got one! Feels like a sunfish." Grandpa straightened up in his chair, set the hook, and began to slowly reel in his catch. I watched from my position on the edge of the grass as the four-inch sunfish dangled from the line before landing on his lap. "Yep, I knew it. They never put up a fight." He admired the speckles of green and gold for a moment, seemingly out of respect, before tossing it back into the water with a *there ya go*.

As Grandpa rethreaded a new worm on his hook, I felt a heavy tug on my pole. While I knew this was no sunfish, I couldn't help but assume I'd likely let out the line too far and caught the bottom. I set the hook and began reeling it in without much fight. I stepped up to the water's edge and an algae-covered branch emerged on the end of my line.

Dang it. "Just a branch," I told Grandpa who was chuckling as his arthritic ridden fingers struggled with his hook and worm. "Let me help you with that."

"How embarrassing... I've been baiting worms for 75 years and now I can barely hold the hook still. Don't you go getting old, Lucas. This ain't no way to live."

"Don't worry, Grandpa. I'll be sure to die young and leave a good-looking corpse."

We both laughed together as I finished baiting his hook. From the corner of my eye I studied his liver spots, his sagging skin, the dark bags under his eyes, and the tubes that fed him oxygen through his nose. In a way, he was right about getting old. But nobody really wants to die young, do they?

"All set, cast 'er out."

"Thanks, Lukie. You're a good man, ya know?" he said, gently tapping me on the shoulder.

I placed my hand atop his and gave it a warm squeeze. "Alright, alright. Enough of that mushy shit. Catch me some dinner, Grandpa!"

He let out a belly laugh triggering a phlegmy coughing fit. He spit out a loogie, drew back his pole and let out a long cast that made a splash halfway across the pond. "Ya see that one?" he asked me, his gray eyes shimmering with pride.

"Helluva cast, old timer!"

I kneeled down to remove my catch and rebait my hook. The worm winced as the barb pierced through his slimy cuticle. This part always made me feel terrible, but I'd never let Grandpa know I was such a softie. The idea of a sharp hook piercing through my flesh and guts made me squirm, well, like a worm.

"Whoa now, I think I gotta 'nother one!" Grandpa sat upright in his chair and waited a moment before setting the hook.

"Damn, gonna leave something for me to catch or you going to empty the whole pond?" I japed.

"Well, I don't know what this is. Might be another stick fish."

The joke was not lost on me. The old man still had his witty sense of humor even if his body was losing the battle against time. I loved that about him. Just then the groundskeeper from before pulled up onto the lawn behind us, dropped his mowing deck, and started on the lawn seemingly still listening to his music. He noticed us and shot me a wave, so I waved back. do

"It's not fighting back, but it feels kinda heavy. What'n the hell could it be?"

The line zigzagged through the water before finally surfacing from beneath the dark pond. A garland of weeds dangled from his catch. Trickling drops of water broke the mirror-like reflection of the trees branches above.

He brought it onto the lawn and whipped it in my direction, slapping me in the face with the wet weeds.

"Thanks for that..."

He laughed out loud before apologizing. "What do we got there?" He asked, lowering it to the green grass.

I kneeled down and began plucking off the tangle of hydrilla. Just as I was about to say I wasn't sure what it was when I spotted it: a human tooth. No, a set of human teeth.

Disgusted, I winced and fell back onto my hands in a crabwalk position. "What's wrong with you? What is it, Luke?"

"I—I don't know... I think it's a jaw."

"A what now? There ain't no jawfish in here? Those are—"

"Not a jaw*fish*, Grandpa, a *jaw*. Like—a human jaw."

He stared at me wide-eyed. Either he didn't know what to say or he was contemplating how on Earth a human jaw could end up in a pond beside the VA hospital.

"Well, bring it here. I want to see it up close."

"I ain't touchin' that thing! You crazy?" I stood back up and wiped my hands on my pants knowing the damage had been done. Dead things made me squeamish.

Grandpa scoffed at this then lifted his pole so the jaw would swing towards him. It landed in his lap, and he finished cleaning off the weeds so he could get a better look. Sure enough, it was a human jaw with a full set of algae-covered teeth.

"Guess the guy never heard of floss," Grandpa burst into laughter at his own joke.

"Grandpa, this isn't funny. We gotta tell someone about this."

"Tell who? I ain't getting mixed up in some drawn out murder trial. I don't have much time left, Lucas. Let sleeping dogs lie. I say we throw it back and forget we ever saw it."

"How noble of you..."

The groundskeeper pulled up on his mower and parked a few yards away from us. He dropped the throttle and removed his headphones.

"Hey fellas, not accusing ya of anything but I did just see the rent-a-cops headin' this way. You may want to put away those poles before you get a fine."

We both nodded and thanked him, trying to conceal the piece of human we'd found.

"You guys catch anything good?"

"Nah, not really. Just a sunner—"

"And a big ol' stickfish," Grandpa interjected with some more of his witty humor.

"Stickfish? Bahaha that's a good one! Well just wanted to give you guys a heads up. Don't want you getting into no trouble on this beautiful day."

"Thanks a lot, man. We appreciate that. Have a good day!" I said, hoping he'd get the hint.

"You both as well," he said, giving me a wink. I couldn't help but notice his eyes shift for the briefest of moments to Grandpa's lap. Without another word, he gunned the throttle of his zero-turn and continued on with his task.

"What a strange guy..." Grandpa said. We both looked at each other, then laughed again. "Come on, Lukie. Let's toss that thing back before those cops come rolling by. I don't want any trouble. My nurse'll tear me a new asshole if she knew I was fishing over here. The one I got barely works as it is."

I eyed the jaw trying to think of any reasonable explanations for it to be lying at the bottom of the pond of the veteran's hospital. Things weren't adding up. There was something fishy going on here. But Grandpa did have a point. We were fishing in a prohibited location, and we were sure to be wrapped up in months if not years of litigation and investigations. Grandpa didn't have years.

"You're right. Let sleeping dogs lie. We don't need to get involved in whatever this is." I walked over to a loose maple leaf that had fallen on the ground and picked it up. "Here, let me see it." With the leaf, I pinched the jaws between my fingers, walked up to the water's edge and chucked it back into the water as far as I could.

"Good throw, Lukie. Now let's put that behind us. What do ya say we go to the cafeteria and grab some chow?"

"Sounds good, Grandpa. I could go for a bite to eat."

§

Lunch came and went while I sat with Grandpa in the courtyard chatting about my new case manager position with the drug court. All the while, the only thing I could think of was the jawbone. Something just wasn't sitting right with me. I could tell Grandpa had all but forgotten about it since I tossed it back into the pond. A benefit of his advanced age was his inability to remember much of anything from the present. He could tell you who won the 1956 World Series or the make and model of his first car, but there was a slim chance he would remember anything about our current conversation.

I followed him back up to ward 7C and buzzed him in. After a few moments, a nurse opened the door, pretended not to recognize Grandpa, then with a warm smile let us in. That same potent odor of sick elderly people hit as we passed through the door, and pangs of guilt jolted through my chest for leaving Grandpa alone in this place.

I helped him up into his bed and he fell back onto his pillow with a loud exaggerated exhale.

"Hey Lukie, turn on the game, wouldja? Sox are playing the Orioles." His breathing was labored, and I could tell he wouldn't be awake ten minutes after I left.

"Sure, Grandpa." I did so, and over the voice of the commentators I told him I had a great time fishing with him, that I loved him, and that I would see him in a couple weeks.

"I'm proud of you, Lukie. I really am," he said, placing a big hand on my knee. "You're going to do great things in your lifetime. I know it to be true. I just hope I'm around to see it."

"Don't you worry about that. You'll be around for a long time, Grandpa. I'll see you real soon." I patted his hand and kissed him on the forehead. "See you real soon."

As I was riding down the elevator, the vision of the jawbone passed through my mind. Green algae coating each tooth. Pieces of pond weed rooted in between toothy gaps. I knew if there was a jawbone there had to be more pieces of body down there. More remains. But who did they belong to?

DING

The doors to the elevator opened, quickly pulling me from my mental forensic analysis. As I stepped out completely distracted, I walked directly into someone waiting to go up. To my surprise, it was the groundskeeper that had saved us from being busted by the VA police.

"Whoa now, you almost ran me over," he said jokingly.

"Wow, my apologies, man. I was a bit distracted."

"No worries at all. You sayin' goodbye to your father?"

"Grandfather, actually. And yes. It's always tough leaving him behind."

"Oh I imagine it is. You just never know when it'll be the last time," he winked at this. "But don't you worry. Those ladies up there are top notch. The best the VA has to offer. I'm sure you'll have plenty more opportunities to catch them stickfish. Well, gotta run. Enjoy your day."

I thanked him and stepped out of his way. He was nice enough, but his awkward demeaner made me uneasy and his toothy grin as the elevator closed didn't help.

§

A few days passed since I left Grandpa to his ball game, and I hadn't stopped thinking about our grim discovery. I would be leaving to get settled in at the dorm in a few months. I knew there was no way I could possibly sit on the information for that long, let alone until after Grandpa passed. The latter was something I hated to think about, but this reality became more obvious after our day at the pond. His life was slipping away from him, and he wouldn't be able to hang on much longer. It crushed me to think of him passing while I was away at school.

I'd been thinking about Grandpa's inevitable passing a lot which shifted my thoughts back to our macabre catch. I wondered what else was hiding in that pond. A skull? A rib cage? An entire body? I *had* to know. A quick trip to the sporting goods store and I was ready to find out.

I decided to go on a Thursday night. I parked a mile away off the main road and with my newly acquired back pack, I followed the powerlines that led to some of the walking trails surrounding the hospital grounds. The sun was setting rapidly, and I worried I wouldn't reach the pond before darkness fell. As luck would have it, I found the pond just as the street lights were kicking on. The timing was perfect.

I looked around to make sure the coast was clear. Other than a few employees leaving work for the night, the grounds were quiet. I set down my pack behind a fallen log and pulled out a set of professional-grade scuba goggles, a snorkel, an extendable hook, and lastly a waterproof spotlight.

The water was warmer than expected and I took to the snorkel surprisingly fast. Using the spotlight as my guide, I slowly made my way to the vicinity of the pond where Grandpa hooked onto the jaw. The water had a greenish hue to it due to all the algae, but overall it was fairly clean and free of any litter.

I scanned the bottom with the spotlight for ten minutes or so and had almost given up hope until a set of dark, hollow eyes peeked out at me from behind a rock. I gasped into the snorkel, almost gagging myself. It was a skull. I moved closer to get a better look, assuming I'd found a match for the jawbone. I was dead wrong. Not only did the skull have a jaw, but the entire skeleton was also tangled amongst the weeds. Using the hook, I poked at them to get a better look. I noticed half the leg was missing below the knee.

146

An amputee. Then I found the second body. This one was missing an entire arm below the shoulder. Thick algae had coated every bone making it look like some strange green alien species.

After a good twenty minutes, I'd discovered close to nine bodies. The last one was missing its jaw. I swam back to shore and welcomed a mouthful of fresh air. I felt dirty. Swimming with corpses will do that to a person. I climbed up onto the edge of the pond and sat down to catch my breath, still wearing my goggles and snorkel. I collapsed the hook and let it dangle from my wrist by the vinyl loop.

I had no idea what to do next. Where was I supposed to go with this information that would involve me admitting to trespassing, fishing in a prohibited waterway on federal property, and Lord knows what other crimes? Was it really worth it? I'd be risking so much to gain so little. That's when I heard it.

Click.

I'd seen enough movies to know what the cocking of a pistol sounded like.

"Don't fucking move, asshole," a familiar voice ordered in a menacing tone. I sat, paralyzed with fear. "You couldn't leave well enough alone could you? You just *had* to come snooping around where you didn't belong?"

"Look, man. I didn't see *anything.* I was looking for my grandfather's watch. He thought he might have dropped it in here the—" my words cut off by the feeling of hard steel on the back of my head.

"Stop talking. I saw you guys out here yesterday. Remember? Or did you already forget how I saved your asses from getting busted?"

"The groundskeeper?"

"Bingo!" he said, pressing the barrel of his sidearm harder into my skull reasserting his dominance. "I knew what you two were up to. What you'd found. I thought we had an unspoken understanding but that's what I get for putting my faith in strangers."

"Look, I'm not sure what you're talking about. We went fishing. That's it. I appreciate you helping us out. Now please, put down the gun—"

"I'll make the demands here. Stand up," he said, again putting excessive pressure on the back of my head.

I tried my best to remain calm. I'd never be in this type of situation. I started to imagine what Grandpa would have done. The seasoned war veteran who'd been reduced to a withering old man by the cruel passage of time. How would he handle someone holding a gun to his head?

I got to my feet. The heft of my wet clothes weighing me down made it tougher than it should have been. I kept my eyes to the ground in an attempt to look intimidated. Truth was, I had no idea what this maniac was capable of.

"Good, now walk. Make any sudden moves, and I'll blow your fucking head off."

I did as I was told. It was hard to see where I was going through my goggles, so I kept my steps high and hoped I didn't trip.

"Now that the secret is out, would you mind telling me who those bodies belong to?" I asked, hoping that getting him to talk might delay the inevitable. Something I'd learned from television and movies was that crazy people always liked to talk about their crimes.

"Who do you think, Sherlock? They were patients. I didn't kill them if that's what you're thinking. It's the fucked up bureaucracy that brought them to me."

"What is that supposed to mean?" I said, almost tripping on a rotting log.

"What it means is this hospital pretends to provide the utmost care to our nation's *finest* but it's all a façade." There was a hint of sarcasm in his tone as it shifted from one of control to one of mockery. I had to tread lightly so as not to piss him off enough to pull the trigger. I still had to come up with a plan to get out of this mess. "These men all died alone in hospice after *bravely* murdering innocent poor people for their country. And what do you think happened after they died? A parade? A festival thrown in their honor?"

I remained silent.

"They call the fucking groundskeeper to pick up their decrepit old bags of flesh and bone to drop off at the morgue. Just like taking out the trash. The morticians don't even care enough to follow up with the wards. I had my fun then tossed their bodies where they wouldn't be found. What do you think of that?"

I could feel a pang of anger welling up inside my chest. The idea of Grandpa being left in the hands of this piece of shit—to be handled like a dirty diaper—made me sick. I decided then and there I would have to find a way to use this anger.

"I asked you a fucking question, dickhead. How does that make you feel knowing that tomorrow I'll be hauling out your grandpappy like a big bag of garbage?"

I gritted my teeth. I slowly maneuvered my hand to the handle of the hook.

"What are you talking about?"

"You haven't figure it out yet, dumbass? I'm going to kill you out here in these woods, then tomorrow I'm going to smother that old bastard with a pillow until he stops breathing and shits in his Depends."

With a flick of the wrist, I extended the hook and swung it back hitting him on the wrist, knocking the gun from his hand. A rustle of the bushes as the sidearm hit the ground reassured me he was unarmed. Stunned by the sudden attack, he didn't move as I swung again, catching him on the side of the face. I tried pulling back the hook, but it was caught on something. I yanked it back again and felt something tear as he let out a gargled cry of pain.

He tried talking but sounded like he was choking on something. I hauled back, took one more powerful swing, aiming lower this time. I felt something rupture as the end of the hook caught him in the midsection. I stood there for a moment as the gargling cries died off. I thought again of the worms and how we punctured their fleshy bodies and wondered what it must feel like to be stuck to the end of a hook. I supposed I could ask this guy.

I removed the goggles letting them hang off my neck alongside the snorkel. I took a moment to gather my composure, trying to cope with the fact that I just murdered a madman with a telescoping boat hook. Not exactly how I planned to spend my evening.

It took longer than expected to drag his body through the woods back to the pond. I was not familiar with how to properly dispose of a dead body, but as they say, when in Vegas.

I decided it would be poetic justice to dispose of his dead body the same way he did those fallen heroes. I filled his clothing with as many heavy rocks as I could fit before dragging his body into the pond. Of course I knew that meant I would never be given the chance to alert the authorities of the desecrated bodies that littered the bottom of the pond. That bothered me more than ridding the world of this piece of garbage. But as Grandpa once said, let sleeping dogs lie.

UNHOLY COMMUNION

Sunday Mass at Saint Januarius always ended at precisely 11:25am. The congregation would gather their belongings, make their way to their preferred exits, and walk to their cars. Many of them met at a nearby diner for lunch. The others returned to their homes and sat in front of the television to catch afternoon mass on cable access. The rest quietly waited near the gold-trimmed ivory stoup for Father Sanglait's direction to the activities basement.

I waited for the last few old fogies to shuffle their way down the stairs, then for the Father to give me a thumbs up—I assumed he thought it made him look hip—change out of my... whatever they were called—I just called them robes. Hot as Hell is what they really were. Kind of ironic, ain't it?

Cranking up Pearl Jam on my Walkman, I grabbed my bike from behind the dumpster. Nothing made me feel more alive than loud music while cruising on my BMX—especially coasting down Church Street at 100mph. I thought about grabbing a slice at Gerard's Pizza. After lunch, I would head down Main Street to Downtown Comics & Tabletop Games to see if Jeff had gotten in any new D&D figurines. I needed a replacement for the archer my dog chewed. Not to mention I was getting sick of using the Candyland piece and being teased by the guys.

However, on this particular day—which happened to be my last day as an altar boy—I made a grave mistake. My grandmother asked me to retrieve her casserole dish that she left behind at the previous bean supper. She made her famous green bean casserole—between you and me, it was just the recipe printed on the back of a cream of mushroom can. When I grabbed my bike, threw on my backpack, turned up the tunes, and started down the dirt path, I'd passed through the park before remembering the dish. *Good thing I hadn't made it all the way down to Main Street.* Church Street is a long steep hill, and I wasn't in the mood to walk my bike back up it, even on a cooler than normal July day.

No biggie, so I turned around and headed back to the church. This time I parked my bike beside the front steps. I would just be in and out anyway, at least I thought.

The entrance was unlocked, typical for Catholic church on a Sunday. Once mass was over and the congregation had done their due diligence, by saying their prayers, accepting their communion, and hailing their Marys, they'd be off the hook for another seven days. Their passage through the gates of heaven solidified in case something sinful happened between Sundays. It was all a load of crap to me, but I wanted to do right by my family for as long as necessary. Catholics are kind of hardcore when it comes to tradition. I mean, honestly, what thirteen-year-old worries about life after death when they *have* so much life ahead of them?

I pushed open the enormous door. The empty pews looked so creepy. The large cross that hung behind the presider's chair looked more ominous than when I was up there on the sanctuary during mass. Thankfully, the lights behind the stage were off, and I did my best to avoid Jesus' mournful gaze. I was overcome with guilt every time I looked up at his face, but since I didn't need to enter the sanctuary, Jesus would have to wait until next Sunday to see me again. My business was in the basement.

I passed through the lobby. It was littered with prayer pamphlets, bulletin boards holding up calendars of upcoming events, collection envelopes, and all sorts of junk. The scent of old lady perfume hung heavy in the air, masking the undertone of something... different. I couldn't quite put my finger on it at first, but it wasn't pleasant.

I walked down the stairs humming the melody to *Oceans,* my favorite track from the *Ten* album. The further I went in my descent, the stronger the smell became. I still couldn't pinpoint what the smell was, but in my naivety, I assumed it was a casserole left out to spoil. Something I wanted nothing to do with.

I reached the basement and made my way towards the kitchen, hopeful that the dish would be resting in the dish rack to dry. Wrong. I began opening and closing cabinet after cabinet searching for my Grandmother's dish. Four cabinets later, I finally found one labeled *Dolores*. I lifted it out, slid it into the large pocket of my backpack, zipped it shut then closed the cabinet. Pulling the straps over my shoulders, I faintly heard the chanting.

The sounds sent goosebumps all over my skin. I'd never heard anything like it. This went way beyond the creepy, cult-like mantra chanting of typical Catholic mass. It almost sounded like the antithesis of the hymns sung in unison during Sunday masses. The chanting had an otherworldly harmony and an eerie melody that reminded him of an old movie I'd seen where a man was burned alive in a massive effigy. There was even an out-of-tune organ playing in the foreground. This wasn't a song I recognized and part of me knew it was something blasphemous. There was no way I was going to leave that basement without having a peek.

The dish weighed down my shoulders a bit, but it wasn't too bad. I tightened the shoulder straps as I turned left out of the kitchen and slowly made my way through the wood paneled hallway. I was officially the furthest I'd ever been into the basement seeing as the catechism room and dining hall were both before the kitchen. It all looked the same to me, but the music was considerably louder. My growing unease gave in to the illusion that the hallway was getting smaller, and the walls were closing in around me. Of course this wasn't true, but no one could tell me that.

The further down the hall I walked, the more I could understand the singing.

Tiptoeing down the corridor, I kept asking myself what they could be doing. This was not one of the many Catholic hymns I had memorized. It was something else. Approaching the door, I recognized the putrid smell that permeated the hallway. My dad got too close to a bonfire one night while roasting a marshmallow and singed the hair on his arm. The smell was burning hair.

I realized what I was doing was stupid. I knew I had no business going any further, but I was young, dumb, and my curiosity got the better of me. The music was hypnotic. I felt like it was pulling me in, and I couldn't leave if I wanted to.

The door at the end of the hallway—which was normally locked—was now ajar. Every church has that one room that always remains locked—this was ours—yet, here it was.

Being careful to control every footfall to keep from making any sound, I crept to the doorway. The sound of the hymnal reverberated off the thin paneling.

I peeked through the narrow gap of the doorway, gasping at what I saw. The congregants who'd stayed behind were kneeling in rows on the floor. Their arms hung down to their sides with their palms facing out. They were chanting while a woman played an unfamiliar song on the organ. Up front, a man was presumably receiving some sort of communion. I recognized him as Mr. Fournier, my mailman. He stood in front of a malformed version of Father Sanglait. The Father stood on a pedestal black as obsidian. The pedestal was enwreathed in braids of human hair that smoldered like sticks of incense. A set of leathery wings resembling those of a bat stretched out at his sides. His golden garments—which he'd worn during mass that day—were split down the middle exposing his bare chest. A pair of voluptuous, fur-covered breasts hung down from the opening. Mr. Fournier stood with his left hand cupped atop his right, hovering beneath one of the breasts. As he did, the Father squeezed the soft tissue causing the engorged nipple on the left breast to excrete a rose-colored milky liquid. Mr. Fournier nodded, raised his hand to his lips, and drank until his hand was empty.

I gagged. I'd never seen something so disgusting in my life, but that wasn't even the worst of it. As Mr. Fournier stepped back, I could see a trail of coarse hair running down the beast's stomach, encircling a long, pulsing, flesh-colored cord that stretched down to the floor before disappearing behind a velvet curtain draped behind him.

I could sense that behind that curtain lived something far worse than what I was permitted to see. An otherworldly creature resembling something from one of my monster manuals.

I tried not to think about it for too long. I wanted to turn around and get the hell out of that church. I *had* the dish, but I couldn't resist the pull. Something was drawing me in. Something wanted me to see. Was it the organ music, the chanting, my own morbid curiosity, or maybe some unseen supernatural force had taken hold of me? I didn't want to find out.

Mr. Fournier brought his arms to his sides, palms up, and bowed before the beast as it let out a harsh screech resembling something out of a monster movie. The congregants stayed oblivious and on their knees as they listened to the sweetest song they'd ever heard.

From the back of the room, three men stood up. The two older men stood on either side of the younger man. The one in the middle's hands were bound and he was gagged tightly around his mouth. His eyes had a languid, sedation about them.

As the trio made their way through the crowd of the kneeling congregants, it dawned on me where I'd recognized the young man from. I'd seen him regularly under the overpass where he'd set up camp. He was homeless.

My heart raced. I wiped the sweat from my brow as it started to burn my eyes. I didn't want to watch and honestly, I'd later wished that I hadn't. They made their way to the front and the younger man snapped out of his sedation just in time to go face-to-face with the winged beast. The beast flapped its wings sending a warm gust throughout the room. The thin hair of the congregants swayed like autumn grass. The smell was a putrid combination of body odor, spoiled milk and sulfur. The worshippers breathed in the stink as though it was the sweetest bouquet of spring lilacs.

To my relief, the beast covered his exposed torso leaving only the bottom left untucked so the fleshy cord could hang out below. The beast placed a hand on the young man's forehead, recited a prayer in an ancient tongue, before nodding at the other two men who stepped back. He reached down and grabbed the young man's hand with the utmost care. For a moment,

155

holding it like a mother does her child, he escorted the man to a split in the curtains.

The other two men returned to their kneeling positions in the rear of the congregation.

With the curtain closed, I could hear a heavy, lascivious breathing coming from behind it. Whatever it was sounded big. I heard the homeless man's screams cut short by an awful squelchy, crunching sound. Chunks of meat, blood, and pieces of shattered bone cascaded down to the floor, flowing out from behind the curtain in rivers. The blood began to boil as though the floor was the cooking surface of a hot skillet. Dense blood bubbles formed then popped. The sound was sickening.

I keeled over as the contents of my stomach splashed across the floor of the doorway. I knew I'd messed up but there was nothing I could do to stop it. I wiped my chin and slowly looked up from the floor. The entire congregation had turned its attention to me, and their eyes shifted from hues of blues, green, browns and grey to fiery red and orange. In unison, they all flashed their impossibly long teeth at me before letting out a hissing noise.

It was time to leave. I was turning to go when Father Sanglait yanked back the curtain to see what had interrupted the unholy communion. Behind the curtain was a grotesque amalgamation of Jesus Christ as he was imagined on the cross hanging above the stage in the chapel and an indescribable slack-jawed monster. Its ribs protruded from beneath its translucent flesh. Its arms and legs were elongated with cracked knuckles that nearly touched the floor. Its head—topped in a crown of human teeth and severed arteries—brushed the ceiling. The umbilical cord ran up between its thighs and under his burlap sash, tarnished with red and brown stains. Bits and pieces of the homeless man's remains lingered on its chin, neck and chest. I'd only caught a glimpse before Father Sanglait screamed my name—in an inhuman voice teeming with rage. Under his command, the congregation stood up and started their pursuit.

I slammed the door shut and bolted back down the hallway. Just as I reached the stairwell, the door at the end of the hall tore open and dozens of feet scampered after me. I ran up the stairs, skipping every other step to save time. Tripping on the top step, I stumbled head first onto the floor of the lobby, turning just in time to land on my backpack. The solid surface of the casserole dish nearly knocked the wind out of me.

Gasping for breath, I got to my knees and back onto my feet just as a malevolent face rounded the last few steps. It was Mrs. Carmichael, my first-grade teacher.

Passing by the sanctuary, I burst through the heavy doors for the last time, cleared the granite steps with a leap of faith, and landed on the crumbling sidewalk.

I hopped onto my bike and pushed off into the street. As I passed through the wooden fence bordering the park, I took one last look at the church to check on my pursuers. Standing just outside the rusted gates of the Saint Januarius Cemetery was Father Sanglait. To my surprise, he was smiling. An awful, haunting smile that spoke a thousand words. Something inside me sensed this was far from over.

I'd never pedaled so hard in my life. I made it through the park then down Church Hill at 300 mph. I bypassed Gerard's Pizza and went straight to Downtown Comics. I busted in the door and the small bell nearly broke off its hook. A few teenage boys were in the back playing a game of *Magic the Gathering,* and another kid my age I didn't recognize was flipping through the discount comics with Jeff, the clerk. I crashed onto my knees, panting like a dog baking in the summer sun, attempting to catch my breath.

A look of concern and confusion washed over Jeff. He set down the copy of *X-Men* and the other kid stared at me wide-eyed before Jeff approached me.

"Dude, you alright? Excuse me for one second, Connor."

Before he could finish, everything went fuzzy, and I passed out on the floor.

§

Later that afternoon, I brought the casserole dish back to my grandmother. Boy was it fun trying to come up with an excuse as to why it was broken into three pieces. The bruises on my back told the story that she'd never heard. She was only a little mad, but I could tell she was excited about something else that I wasn't privy to. I asked her what was going on and without hesitation, she explained that Father Sanglait had phoned her and asked if she could stay late after mass on Sunday.

SACRIFICE

The lights on the horizon were cajoling Sophie to carry on by offering her a false sense of hope. Still, she had been walking for so long she felt there was no other option. She was malnourished and nearly dehydrated among other physical ailments making the trek near impossible. The brilliant lights in the distance were something to strive for, but she had no idea what she was expecting to find once she reached them.

How many miles had she walked since leaving the dank root cellar at her parent's farm? How long had she been hiding down there feasting on nothing but fermented vegetables and moldy potatoes?

Her memory had become as unreliable as the fuzzy pink slippers that kept slipping off her feet. They were muddied and full of holes, but they helped keep the battered pavement from tearing apart her swollen feet. Her obnoxiously bright yellow rain poncho was much too thin to stop the brutally cold winds from biting at her soft flesh. On her legs she wore sky blue flannel pajama pants and upon her head, a wide-brimmed fishing cap that belonged to her father. If anyone was alive to see her roaming, they may assume she escaped from an asylum.

§

She was tucked into bed on the night the bombs dropped, hence her ill-advised attire. Her parents had insisted on meeting Benjamin before the wedding, so they took a road trip out to their farm in Nebraska to stay for a couple of days.

Sophie wasn't feeling well that evening, so she went to bed early while her fiancé and her parents drove to town for a few drinks. They took the opportunity to get to know each other better at the behest of the bride-to-be.

While Sophie slept, the old tube radio in the living room quietly issued a public service announcement. Sophie woke up with a dry mouth. The house was quiet when she slid her feet into a pair of slippers. As she filled a glass at the kitchen sink the radio emitted a buzzing followed by a voice repeating the pre-programmed PSA. She turned up the volume knob to listen. It was warning people to find shelter immediately.

Still carrying her lukewarm tap water, she stepped outside onto the screened-in porch slightly confused. The truck was still gone. *I hope they're having a good time,* she thought to herself. Taking a sip, she was just in time to see a blinding flash of light off in the distance followed by a ground-shaking concussive explosion.

The glass of water dropped from her hand. As she stared in awe of the horrific sight, she wished she hadn't insisted her family go out. She was all alone, and this was not only a test.

Still in her pajamas, she ran back to her childhood bedroom, reached into a duffle bag and stuffed something into the waist of her pants. Returning to the porch, she pushed open the screen door, stepped into the damp grass and headed towards the root cellar behind the barn. The autumn air was balmy and calming on her clammy flesh. She had no idea what was happening, but obediently heeded the warning from the voice on the radio.

She struggled to lift the heavy door to the root cellar but managed to get it open. As her slippered foot landed on the top step she was greeted with a familiar smell. She often played down there as a child to escape the summer heat.

With a brief hesitation she looked back at the house, then at the direction of the flash. Conflicted, her heart sank though she knew she had no other choice. Sophie started her descent into the darkness of the cellar. The heavy door slammed shut sealing her underground.

When she reached the dirt floor two more explosions went off sounding much closer. Clinking glass from jars of canned food shook all around here. A few shattered as they fell from the shelves. Her hands found candles and a box of matches on a shelf by the stairs. She lit the candle, felt her way to the back corner and in a seated fetal position covered her ears. Then came the silence. The flickering candle was her only light. Then the waiting.

§

"Don't worry, Benny. I won't give up," Sophie said affectionately while she rubbed her protruding belly. "The lights are getting closer by the day and your mom is a tough old gal. And look, I even rescued your first toy," she pulled the plush blue teddy bear out from behind her back.

Holding it out front of her belly, she spoke for the toy in the best teddy bear voice she could muster.

"Hi there, little Benny. We're going to be best friends. My name is Bunky. It's nice to meet you, pal," She tucked it back into her pajamas and pulled the pant strings tight.

Reverting back to her own voice, she said, "Bunky is almost as excited to meet you as I am, Benny. We'll get through this, I promise."

She wasn't being completely honest with her unborn son. She was terrified. Most of her traveling took place at night when the lights were visible on the horizon, and she'd always had a slight fear of the dark. For the first time in a long time she was unsure about her future. She was the type to meticulously plan out every aspect of her life ahead of time, yet here she was. The bombs were a big wakeup call that like her baby, she hadn't planned for.

She hadn't come across a living person the whole trip since leaving Sidney. When she left the cellar, the house was reduced to rubble. Nothing was salvageable.

Heading southwest on Route 113 she had no idea where she was going. Instinctively headed in the direction away from that of the blast seemed like the best bet. She attributed the lack of people to being out in the country, but deep down she knew that wasn't the reason. They were all dead.

Burnt cars were staggered along the highway. Many had driven into the ditch, but many managed to stay on the road. Desperately stopping by each car she came across to scrounge for food or drink. Occasionally, she got lucky and found a half full bottle of water or a can of soda stuffed into a glovebox, but that wasn't often enough.

She started to observe that the further west she traveled, the less damage had been done to the vehicles. Her hope was maybe she'd come across another person or an operational vehicle so she could drive herself the rest of the way but wasn't ready to hold her breath yet.

The bodies were easily the worst part. Most of the bodies and cars were burnt to a crisp. Not a single car she had searched was vacant. A lone driver that was on their way home from work. A couple that went out for dinner and a movie. From time to time she was greeted by an entire family as she opened the blackened door to their minivan.

Windows were smashed in from the concussion of the blast which let some of the smells escape, but not all. Corpses of children in the backseat held toys they refused to share, now melted onto their laps. The parent's skeletal remains with jaws agape as if they had been yelling for their kids to stop bickering; or perhaps screaming for mercy. Even the occasional family dog curled up in a heap of exposed bones and blackened fur in the far back. This chilled Sophie to the bone.

She was reluctant to rummage through the cars at first, but like a starving rat sniffing around a dumpster, she had no choice. It was life or death, and she *was* eating for two after all. The combination of the constant walking and the baby boy growing in her womb made it all the more difficult to carry on without sustenance. The palms of her hands were stained black from the ash she was digging through. Half the time she didn't know if it was organic or synthetic material. She only knew she was desperate for some nourishment.

As dawn approached on the umpteenth day, she noticed a dented green sign slanted on its posts beside the highway. She took a bite from a melted candy bar she found in a glove box and tilted her head to read it.

§

MERINO - 22 MILES
BRUSH - 44 MILES
DENVER - 141 MILES

§

Her shoulders sank in disappointment. She took another bite and with a mouthful of chocolate and nougat said to her son, "If those lights are in Denver, I'm going to need some better shoes, Benny. These slippers won't last much longer," she caressed her belly. "You guys better cross your fingers that I find something in my size within the next few miles."

"Since I don't have fingers, I'll keep my paws crossed," Bunky said.

Sophie smiled at the sincerity in the teddy bear's voice. "Thanks Bunky. I'm sure that still counts."

Her walking speed was hindered by lack of sleep, aching feet and severe hunger pains. The lines on the road seemed to stretch on forever. She tried to count them at one point for a distraction but lost track after a couple hundred.

Although she was exhausted, her main concern was for Benny. As rough as she was having it, he was likely dealing with his own struggle. This realization made her feel terrible. *I'm already failing as a mother before my child is even born.* As much as she wanted to cry, she didn't have the energy nor the fluids to spare.

She wasn't granted enough time to mourn the loss of her family before heading out on the road. Knowing Benny was due any day she didn't want to risk being alone when he decided to join the world; and what a time he'd chosen to be born. This weighed on her conscience as well.

The next vehicle she came across after the sign was a pickup truck. From her vantage point, she saw there was limited damage done to the outside of the truck. As she got closer she could see the shape of a person in the driver's seat. A hairy elbow hung out the window.

"Hello?" She greeted as she timidly rounded the tailgate. "Excuse me?"

No response. The truck had four flat tires. She walked up to the driver's side window to look in.

The man was dead, per usual, but he had no burn marks, and the cab interior was in good shape. In the middle of his forehead was a hole where a trickle of blood dried onto his face. *A bullet hole.* Sophie let out a gasp. *Did he commit suicide? No, people don't shoot themselves in the forehead.* While contemplating the laws of suicide, she peered into the truck beside the man but saw no firearm.

"That's odd," she said. The mysterious murder of the man in the truck made her anxious. Stepping back from the truck she looked around in all directions. No one was in sight, but she knew she was no longer alone.

§

"Will we find some real food soon? I could sure use some honey comb right about now," the teddy bear asked from his rear facing position tucked into her pajama pants.

"I sure hope so, Bunky. I sure hope so. Do bears even eat honeycomb?" She had no idea. "I imagine Benny must be starving right about now." Another pang of guilt forced Sophie to overlook her own suffering.

A short distance up ahead, something large and yellow came into focus just over a small knoll. *A school bus.* She lifted her hat to wipe her brow. *Bingo!* As her hand dropped, she caught a glimpse of a troubling sight. Red, swollen blisters had started to form on her hand. She pulled it up closer to her face so she could get a better look. Cringing, she dropped her hand immediately. The puss and blood filled boils welled up all over her hands were added to her growing list of concerns.

"We need to hurry, Benny. I'm not doing so well."

"What's wrong, Sophie?" Bunky asked.

"I'm not sure, but I'll be fine if we just get to the lights. First we need to check out that bus. There's *got* to be some shoes in there. Maybe even some food"

She looked down at her feet. The slippers had broken down to brown strips of synthetic material wrapped around her feet with an occasional tuft of pink fuzz. Her exposed toes were chewed up and bloodied. A few of her painted toenails had broken off at some point without her noticing.

The landscape hadn't changed much during her trek. Flat farmlands and fields stretched as far as the eye could see. All in ruin. Most of the trees had blown over. Further south she noticed more trees that still stood. She'd passed several farmhouses that were fairly intact, but her time was running too low to search them.

Nearly 30 minutes later, she had finally reached the number 11 school bus. Half the windows were intact and shut while others were blown out with glass glistening on the pavement below.

"Cross your paws, Bunky. Maybe we'll find some salvageable food in a lunch box."

"They're crossed," his reply was slightly eccentric.

"I remember riding the bus to school. There was a boy that used to tease me every day. Jimmy Campbell. He would pull my hair. Call me names. Turns out, he had a crush on me," she smirked at the memory. Then she wondered to herself if Jimmy had survived the blasts. If anyone besides the three of them had survived. Then she remembered the gunshot.

"That's a nice memory," Bunky said.

"Yeah. He was a funny ki—" she paused, rounded the corner and covered her mouth with her hand. A corpse hung out of a window that had been shattered. A little boy. He wore a baseball glove on one hand. His other hand was skin and bone. She noticed his ball cap sitting on the ground below him that read "Brush Beetdiggers". The writing on the side of the bus read **Brush School District RE - 2J**.

"What the hell is a beet digger?" she asked.

"Beets me," Bunky joshed.

Sophie laughed for the first time since the evening she'd spent with her parent's and Benjamin. She missed them so much. Instantly, tears flooded her eyes. She couldn't stop them, nor did she want to. She was hurting and it felt pleasant to cry. To feel something besides physical pain.

She rested her head on her arms against the side of the bus and let it all out. The shadow of the dead little league player hung down beside her as an afternoon sun ray poked its way through the ashy clouds in the sky.

There was no time for this. She had to think of Benny. She had to press on.

She wiped her eyes dry and hobbled on until she came to the folding door which was slightly ajar. She pushed into the middle of the door but was met with resistance. After wiping dust from the long, skinny door window, she cupped her hands up against the glass to peer inside. She saw what blocked the door. Bodies. Bodies of kids that had jammed up as they tried to evacuate the bus.

"Ugh. They must have been scared shitless. Got all jammed up trying to escape. Poor kids," Sophie said. She imagined being a kid again and seeing bombs hit the Earth while Jimmy wiped his boogers on the back of her neck.

She shook the thoughts from her mind then grabbed at the inside of the door to see if it would budge. She let out a loud grunt. Then another as she tugged. A few jerks later with the sounds of snapping bones, she managed to slide the door open. A couple of children's corpses slid out and landed at her feet.

The dead eyes of a young girl looked up at her. Staring. For a brief moment, she saw herself. Her adolescent dead body lay there staring up at her in awe. Then the girl spoke.

"How did you manage to survive? You should be dead! You should be dead! You and your baby should be DEAD!"

"NOOOOO! SHUT UP!" Sophie screamed at her own corpse. Shaking her head, her vision cleared, and she was no longer staring at herself. Just a dead girl with blonde hair, greying flesh and black eyes. "Fuck this."

Reaching in, she started to find footing between the children so she could step up into the bus. At one point, she was forced to step on a corpse causing the heavy-set boy in a football jersey to release putrid smelling gases from his swollen rotted gut. The bodies of decaying children made her ascent up the three steps difficult. It might not have been so bad had she not been 8-½ months pregnant. Her empty stomach mixed with the unmerciful odors of decomposing children made her feel weak in the stomach and the knees.

As she made it to the landing near the driver's seat, the body of the heavy-set boy she'd stepped on rolled down and slammed against the door, closing it tight.

Stepping into the aisle, she peered down to see what she could find. In the front row was an older lady that must have been a teacher. Traipsing over a couple more bodies she traced the lady's legs down to the floor and noticed a pair of New Balance sneakers that were in decent condition.

"Score!" she whooped in excitement. "A fine pair of sneaks." She plopped down beside the corpse, reached down and began to untie one of the shoes.

"Woohoo!" Bunky cheered. "And look over there."

Sophie turned to find a blue cooler sitting in the empty seat across from the teacher as he pulled the first shoe off.

"Double score," Sophie said while she untied the second shoe and slid it off the foot. "Thank you for your contribution."

Lastly, after sliding the socks off the corpse's feet, she bent forward and struggled to peel off her fuzzy slippers. The sores on her feet made her wince in pain and for the first time she saw some toenails were missing.

It was a bittersweet moment. Almost felt sacrilegious to take off the slippers and discard them like trash. They'd carried her for so many miles the past few days and deserved a proper farewell. Yet again, she had no time for this. Uncomfortably, she managed to squeeze the socks, followed by the sneakers, onto her aching feet.

Turning to face the dead teacher she said, "Thanks lady. I'll put these to good-," she paused. Listening intently, thinking for certain she'd heard a voice. "Did you hear that?" she whispered to the slack jawed corpse. The teacher's sunken eye sockets didn't flinch.

"Hello? Is someone there?" a small voice moaned from the rear of the bus.

Sophie snapped her head around at this. "Yes. Yes, I am here. Where are you?"

"I'm in the back row. Ugggh... I don't feel good," the voice clearly belonged to a child. A small hand weakly stuck up from the back row.

Sophie stood, taking her maiden voyage in her new shoes. Minus the soreness and swelling in her feet, it felt like she was walking on a cloud.

"Be careful. You don't know who this person is," Bunky cautioned.

"Oh hush up, you. It's just a kid."

"Who are you talking to? Is someone else with you?" the boy asked followed by a loud, agonizing moan.

"No. It's—no one. Just talking to myself is all. I'm making my way back to you. What's the matter with you? Are you hurt? Can you walk at all?"

"I-I'm not sure. UGH!" the child let out another moan. "I don't think so."

Stepping over strewn backpacks and bodies, the smell grew more potent with rot the further back she went. Sophie plugged her nose and made her way to the last row. This smell was much worse than the burnt cars.

She looked down into the back seat and saw a pathetic sight. A boy in his early teens was lying across the bench seat in the fetal position. Vomit covered the seat in front of him and collected onto the floor. The older puke had started to congeal like a grotesque stalagmite. He'd been here a while.

The sick boy slowly turned to face Sophie with a despondent look on his face. His cheeks were sunken in, and he looked like a living corpse. If he weren't talking, she'd have thought he was dead like the rest of his classmates. He wore a Colorado Rockies jacket that looked to be a hand-me-down.

"I'm sick, lady. You have to get me to a-a hospital."

"Do you have any idea what's happened?"

"All I remember is the bus stopped suddenly, I was knocked unconscious, and everyone started—well they died. All around me," he coughed then dry heaved. "There were explosions, or something. Right? Was it a bomb?"

"I'm not entirely sure myself, I think so. But—" she stopped. She could hear a slight rumbling. Like an engine. She peeked out the back window of the emergency door. Through the dirty window, she could just make out a jeep as it pulled up and stopped directly behind the bus. After a moment, a couple of people stepped out onto the pavement. They were dressed in fatigues; they wore gas masks and brandished rifles. One might have been a shotgun.

"*UGGGGHHH!*" the boy moaned louder this time. "I really need some help, lady. I think I'm dying."

"Shhh! There's someone out there. Keep it down," she swatted her hand downwards at the boy like he was a fly.

Sophie ducked into the seat across from the boy and landed on the corpse of a young blonde girl that hugged a Hello Kitty backpack.

From outside she could hear men. Their voices muffled through their masks. An authoritative voice gave an order as they approached the door.

168

"Let's have a look inside. We kill anything that moves. Can't risk leaving any survivors out here," the guy in charge commanded.

"You got it."

Sophie's eyes grew to the size of cue balls. She was not about to die on this bus.

"Lady, where'd you go?" the sick boy across the aisle asked.

"Shhhh, you wanna get us killed?" Sophie whispered with a sense of urgency.

"Ugh. I need a hospital. Please- I'm just a kid. Maybe they can help us."

Sophie could hear the heavy footfall of boots outside the bus rounding the corner headed towards the front door.

"Please, just- shut- up," she quietly pleaded with an edge to her tone. "You're gonna get us killed."

"Lady—"

"You need to shut him up or he'll get us all killed," Bunky advised.

"Lady, please. I want my mom. Where's my mom? Is she okay?"

Sophie couldn't take it anymore. She'd made it this far. She wasn't going to let this little shit get her and her unborn son killed. This boy was as good as dead anyway.

"Lady, ple—" the boy's final plea for help was cut short by Sophie's firm right hand. She had jumped across the aisle, laid down on top of him with one hand on his mouth, and the other pinched his nose shut. The boy's eyes bulged as a shocked expression came over the exposed part of his face.

Sophie held him down forcefully, not allowing him to let out a peep. Her face was hot with rage. Just a few mumbled grunts as he struggled to intake breath. His eyes never left hers while he started to vomit into her hand. She didn't let up as bile started to squeeze between her fingers and around the edge of her hand. It smelled like formaldehyde.

His weak arms flailed at his side but didn't make contact with Sophie.

Tears formed in the boy's eyes. Sophie began to shed tears of her own.

The boy choked on his vomit as he desperately attempted to take in breaths. Sophie would not let him. She pressed harder on his face, so his head intended the seat.

Sophie could see the masked figure in the rear pass by the window. She was less than two feet away from the man as she lay atop the boy she was murdering. Had he looked in they would have been nearly eye to eye.

With one last weak grunt, the boy's body went limp though his eyes remained open. They stared off into the abyss beyond Sophie's sore-ridden face. One final tear dropped off the bridge of his nose.

Lifting her head up to look around, she could just see the pair of men up near the front of the folding door.

The bus jerked a bit as one of the men pushed on the door. It wouldn't budge. Another jerk, but the door still held. The last time, the taller man kicked as hard as he could at the door, but he was no match for the dead weight of the heavy-set football fanatic that lay stiff against the door.

"Fuck it. There's no one alive in there. We got more miles to cover. I'm calling this one all clear," the first masked man declared. "Let's get moving. I want to reach Sidney by nightfall and clear it out so we can head back to Denver."

The men turned back towards the rear of the bus, walked past the window where Sophie had murdered the sick boy. Her ears followed their movements while her face was buried in the lap of the boy. They climbed back into their Jeep. They fired up the engine, turned on the radio which blasted loud rock music, then continued on their way northeast away from the direction she was headed.

"Jesus. What the fuck is happening? What did I just do?" She asked as she finally removed her hand from the boy's face. His head fell limp to the side and dark crimson vomit trickled out of the side of his mouth. It landed atop the pile of congealed puke on the floor like cherry syrup on ice cream.

Sophie looked at the sick on her hands, sat up quickly then fell back onto the seat with the young girl. She reached over and wiped the vomit from her hand onto the sweatshirt of the dead girl hugging the backpack. It was hard work to remove the thick vomit from her hand. *That kid must have been rotting from the inside out.* She thought. She couldn't escape the putrefied smell.

When she finished, she looked across at the dead boy. She thought of Benny. Would he be ashamed of what his mother had done? She was a murderer, and the weight of the guilt was too much. Her unborn son was an accomplice. Tears began to collect in the bags under her eyes before they rounded over onto her cheeks.

She wished that Bunky would crack a joke, but even he had nothing. She'd never felt more alone.

She took the time needed to regain her composure before she returned to the front of the bus. She opened the blue cooler but only found a half-full bottle of orange Gatorade, moldy bologna sandwiches and a pack of unopened M&Ms sitting in a shallow puddle of water. She contemplated drinking the melted ice but decided against it.

Knowing there was no way she would be able to move the bodies away from the front door in her condition, she returned to the rear of the bus to utilize the emergency door. She looked down at the dead boy covered in vomit. The boy she killed in cold blood. The smell of his death still lingered on her hands.

"I'm sorry I couldn't help you. I'm sorry I killed you," she exhaled a heavy sigh. "I swear I'm not a killer. Just a mother who'll do anything to protect her baby," but she knew that wasn't true. She *was* a killer. This boy had a mother too.

She lifted the bar to release the door and a loud buzzer sounded which pierced her ears.

Her aching feet pounded onto the pavement as she dropped down from the emergency exit at the rear. This sent a jolt of pain up her legs that almost made her collapse. She turned hastily, afraid someone might hear the buzzer, then rounded the bus and continued on her journey. She had no idea how much further she had to go, but now she couldn't stop no matter how hopeless things seemed. Benny needed her to go on.

§

The hunger pains were becoming unbearable. She'd gone days without real food. Her lips were split and bloodied from dehydration. Her legs felt like they were being stabbed by pins and needles and her feet throbbed. The luxury of the new shoes wore off fast. Benny felt so heavy; like she had an anvil strapped to her waist. The extra bulge on her hips hurt her so bad that even the extra weight of Bunky was unbearable. She started to carry him.

Throughout the night she could see the lights were very close now. The damage over the last 20 miles or so was minimal and the cars were scarcer. She hoped and prayed to find something to eat but had no luck. She had walked so far but still no help had come.

"I wish I could help you bear the load. I really do," Bunky punned, sounding more drained than ever.

Sophie raises the bear up to her face. "You're a real hoot you know that? I hope Benny has your sense of humor."

The bear hung limp in her hands and did not respond. His fur was matted with dirt. One of his plastic beady eyes had come loose and dangled by a thread. Sophie felt like she too was dangling by a thread.

She lowered her companion back down to her side, then saw another sign in the distance. This one was standing upright.

§

BRUSH - 5 MILES
DENVER - 95 MILES

§

"Benny—Benny we're so close! The lights weren't from Denver. They were from a town—," a sharp pain in her abdomen brought her to her knees. She let out a painful moan and clutched at her belly. Bunky fell face first onto the pavement. "No, Benny. Not yet. We...we need to make it to the town first. Ugh. We'll die out here!"

She garnered all the strength she could, picked up the teddy bear, then pulled herself back up onto her feet. The first step was the hardest and the second wasn't much easier.

She pressed on. For her son. For Bunky. For Benjamin. For her parents. For all those who died when the bombs dropped. For the boy she killed.

She was alive, and that was something worth living for.

What should have only taken an hour or two took four. She had no idea what time of day it was when she stepped onto the offramp to head into the

172

town of Brush. Her heart leapt as she stepped onto Colorado Ave and saw a blue H sign. There was a hospital in this town.

"Look, Benny...a hospital." But were there any survivors? She stopped for just a moment to catch her breath. The incline of the offramp was just steep enough to sap her of the little energy that remained in her. Her tank was officially on empty.

She fell into the middle of the road. Her knees hit the pavement which caused her to wince in pain. She was fighting the exhaustion, but it was gradually robbing her of consciousness. Her eyelids felt like they weighed ten pounds apiece.

Bunky lay at her side on the cold pavement as she rolled over and stretched out onto her back. She was so close, but she had nothing left.

The sound of an approaching engine drew nearer. She was barely aware of the oncoming vehicle. She turned to look. Soon footsteps approached her as she faded into a deep sleep.

§

As dreams go, she was back at her apartment in Chicago. She stood up from the toilet holding a pregnancy test. It read positive. Though she was overcome with joy, she hoped that her boyfriend would be just as happy. They hadn't planned for a child, yet she had assured him that she'd taken the proper precautions. Still, sometimes these things happen.

She took a deep breath, let it out, and walked down the hallway towards the kitchen. The morning sunlight shone in through the window at the end of the corridor. A thin stick of incense was burning and giving off a smell of tranquility. The scent put her at ease, and she felt serene.

Benjamin was hovering over the stove tossing scrambled eggs in a cast iron skillet. He hadn't had time to shave yet, so his face was covered in a thick layer of stubble that Sophie thought was sexy. The rest of the room felt hazy to her. Her only focus was on her boyfriend and the plastic strip in her hand that she hid behind her back. The rest of the room was tucked away in her memory.

Benjamin looked up at her as she approached. He shot her a smile.

"Hey babe. Breakfast is almost ready. I hope you have an appetite," Benjamin said.

"Smells delish!" Sophie replied. "I should have a good appetite. I'm eating for two after all," she anxiously smirked, waiting for him to throw the pan of eggs against the wall.

Ben smiled. His mind processed what she had just said. He stopped stirring then dropped the spatula. He slowly gazed up at Sophie with a glint in his eye.

"What do you mean? Are you—?"

Sophie slid out the pregnancy test from behind her back and showed Benjamin the small window that displayed the plus sign. Her expression was anxious. A look of shock formed on his face followed by a bright white smile.

She thought he'd never looked so handsome since they'd met.

"No way! You're kidding me?" he asked in a high-pitched voice accentuated with excitement.

"I would never!"

He wrapped his arms around her waist, lifted her up and twirled her in a circle in the rays of the morning sunlight. The eggs started to burn on the stove but neither cared.

"That's absolutely amazing! I love you so much!" said Benjamin.

"I love you too, Hun. I'm so glad you're happy."

"Of course I'm happy. You just made me the happiest man on Earth. We're going to be parents! I'm going to be a dad!"

He continued to twirl her around on the linoleum floor of their small apartment kitchen. Until suddenly, he stopped. Bending down, he carefully laid her onto the chilly floor. She was confused by this. Bent over her, he peered into her eyes.

"Why'd you leave without me, Sophie?"

"Huh? What do you mean?" she asked.

"You left me and your parents behind. To die!" His voice started to deepen and sound hoarser. "You—just—left us! Didn't even look back!" His skin started to turn red and blister like he was sitting in an oven.

Sophie was terrified. She didn't remember this happening in her memory.

"Ben! What's happening?"

His whole body suddenly became engulfed in flames which singed Sophie's fine arm hair and her eyebrows.

"You're hurting me, Ben!"

His eyeballs popped like kernels of popcorn spewing aqueous humor onto her chest. His skin started to drip off his face exposing his muscle and sinew covered skull.

"Nooo!" Sophie screamed in terror. She flipped over onto her stomach attempting to crawl away from her boyfriend but was stopped by another nightmarish sight.

The young boy from the bus was lying under the kitchen table on his stomach. He picked his head up off the floor to look at Sophie. Blood began to leak from his eye sockets.

"Help me. Please help me," he pleaded as a small hand reached out for her and grabbed her wrist. "Why did you kill me, lady? Why did you kill me?" Projectile vomit exited his mouth hitting Sophie in the face and he started to choke. The heat from Ben burned the back of her neck and she felt her hair ignite in flames. The pain was ungodly.

"NOOO!" Sophie screamed for mercy.

§

Sophie woke from her nightmare. A bright light shone in her eyes from above. Squinting, she looked down at the discomfort that tugged at her arm. There was an IV attached to her festering forearm. She looked around the room she was in. A white curtain was hanging to her right. A mechanism of sorts was sitting to her left.

"You were severely dehydrated and malnourished when they brought you in," a female voice said from the foot of the hospital bed. Sophie hadn't even noticed her there.

Sophie looked down to see a nurse seated in a chair holding a paperback.

"Where—am I?"

"East Morgan County Hospital in Brush. You're in a safe zone now. A couple saw you passed out on Colorado Ave. They picked you up when they saw you were pregnant. Almost ran ya right over. They thought you were

175

dead," the nurse casually explained with no effect. "You're lucky you weren't killed or kidnapped. There's rumors of a militia group on the roads taking people out. *Why?* Who the hell knows?"

This didn't interest Sophie.

"Bunky! My teddy bear. Where is my—" she looked at the rolling bed table and saw Bunky laying on his back.

"They brought him as well. I cleaned him up as best I could. Even sewed up his loose eyeball. Figured it musta been important if you carried it with ya."

Sophie let out a sigh of relief and rested her head back on the pillow. The nurse replaced her bookmark and folded her copy of *The Stand* into her lap.

"You really should rest, miss. You're still in critical condition and had severe radiation poisoning among other things. You barely survived the surgery for Christ sakes."

Sophie furled her brow at this.

"Surgery? What surgery?"

"Your caesarean. You were practically in labor when they found you on the ro—"

Sophie shot her hands down to her belly then sucked in air through her teeth as she felt the pain from her c-section shoot up to her shoulders.

"Benny? Where's my baby?" Her voice shifted to a high-pitched tone of desperation.

The nurse hesitated. For the first time, her voice sounded empathetic.

"I'm really sorry, miss. Your son, uh- Benny, was unresponsive after you gave birth. They tried like hell to help him, but he was just too weak. You're lucky to have made it this far yourself, but I'm afraid Benny didn't survive."

Sophie could feel the nausea welling up in her gut. She refused to come to terms with what the nurse was telling her.

"No...No...No that can't be," she violently shook her head at the nurse. "We made it here. I walked so far, and...WE MADE IT!" Her bloodshot eyes overflowed with tears, stinging the burst boils on her cheeks as they slid down her once beautiful face.

Sophie threw off the thin hospital blanket and swung her legs out, wincing as she was struck by the pain of her recent surgery. The sight of her swollen, sore-covered legs protruding below her hospital gown though shocking, was the least of her worries.

"Benny, I'm coming. Mama's coming! You can't be...Please," the sudden eruption of shock to her heart sent her crumbling to the floor, taking with her the electrocardiogram that was attached to her body.

The nurse jumped up from her seat, dropping her paperback and clipboard to the ground. She rushed over and helped Sophie back onto her bed without uttering a word. Sophie set her head back onto the flimsy hospital pillow.

There was nothing else she could do. She'd beaten the odds. Given all she had to make it this far. The revelation of Benny's death robbed her of any joy she might have felt about her own survival. Like any mother, Sophie would have gladly taken his place had she been given the choice. She watched the green line on the electrocardiogram.

Bunky lay still on the table beside her. His blue fur was spotless. His beady plastic eyes stared blankly at the ceiling tiles of the maternity ward. Sophie reached out and picked him up. The teddy's soft fur between her fingers was familiar and comforting. He smelled fresh. Clutching Bunky to her chest, Sophie gently stroked his blue fur and stared blankly at the ceiling, quietly humming a lullaby.

"I'm so sorry, Benny. Mama loves you."

Thank you so much for reading Hunger For Death.

This collection is my debut attempt at the short story format, and I love the way it came together. All but two of the stories you've read here were written specifically for this collection. "A Trailer Park Christmas" was originally published in the Christmas charity anthology *Santa Claws is Coming to Deathlehem* for Grinning Skull Press. It was my first ever story acceptance and it'll always be special to me. "Sacrifice" was previously published in the *Alien Agenda 2020 Sampler* which was my first anthology invite. The fact that anyone has bought and read *any* of my work means the world to me. I started writing in February of 2020 and since then, it's taken over my life. I've made so many friends, acquittances, and fans and I'm grateful for each and every one. I have more projects in the works including my debut novel, my contribution to the FrightVision series, and several anthologies I'm taking part in.

I'm excited to see what the future holds. I hope you'll join me on this wild ride.

From the bottom of my heart, thank you!

As always, reviews are encouraged and help me out so much!

Thank you!

ACKNOWLEDGEMENTS

First and foremost, I want to thank my family for their unwavering support of my writing. My wife Aryn not only reads all my stories and offers constructive feedback, but she also gifted me or inspired the idea for a couple of the stories in this collection. (I won't say which ones.)

Thanks to author Lydia Prime for her fantastic editing skills and feedback. She has been a lifesaver and played a major role in helping me get this collection out to the world after some unforeseen hindrances.

Thanks to author Todd Keisling for his impressive interior formatting skills. Todd is not only a friend, but he is an extremely talented author having been nominated for a Bram Stoker Award in 2020 for his stellar novel *Devil's Creek,* one of my personal favorite reads of 2020.

Thanks to author Freddie Åhlin for his amazing design on the wrap around cover, Neal Auch for his beautifully macabre photography that graces the front cover, and Brian Scutt for designing the eye-catching front cover.

Thanks to author Brandon Scott who saw my potential as an author and even though things didn't work out with the original publisher, he stuck with me becoming a friend and a mentor.

And finally, to each and every reader that has ever bought or read one of my books. You're helping this guy achieve his dreams and for that, I'm forever grateful!

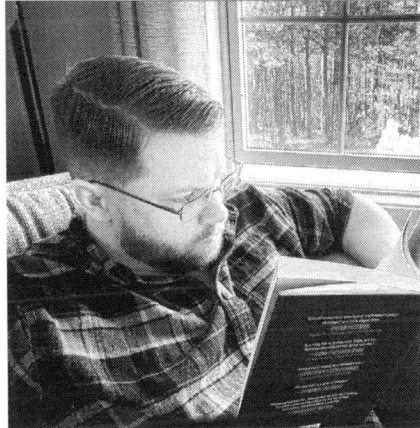

ABOUT THE AUTHOR

JOSHUA MARSELLA is a Maine native. He started writing his first novella *Scratches* during the height of the 2020 Coronavirus pandemic and hasn't stopped since. He lives with his wife, Aryn, and their two sons, Lucca and Lennon, in his hometown. He served in the US armed forces including a tour of duty in Mosul, Iraq from 2004-2005. He later went on to attend The University of Maine at Augusta where he graduated with his bachelor's degree in Mental Health and Human Services in 2016. Since then he's worked as a stay-at-home dad which is when he started writing at night.

Thus far he has written two novellas, *Scratches* and *Severed*, his debut collection, *Hunger For Death,* several short stories in various anthologies, as well as contributing to the FrightVision middle grade horror series. He has no plans to stop writing and looks forward to keeping his readers entertained for as long as he can.

CONTENT WARNINGS

This collection contains themes of violence, gore, sexual assault, injury detail, neglect, child abuse, animal cruelty & death, suicide, death, religion, cannibalism, substance abuse, death of a child, and violence.

Some scenes may be triggering. Please proceed with caution.

Made in the USA
Middletown, DE
25 September 2022

11090067R00104